NEW YORK REVIEW BOOKS
CLASSICS

T0017542

LITTLE SNOW LANDSCAPE

ROBERT WALSER (1878–1956) was born into a German-speaking family in Biel, Switzerland. He left school at fourteen and led a wandering, precarious existence while writing poems, novels, and vast numbers of the "prose pieces" that became his hallmark. In 1933 he abandoned writing and entered a sanatorium—where he remained for the rest of his life.

TOM WHALEN is a novelist, short-story writer, poet, critic, and the co-editor of the Robert Walser issue of the *Review of Contemporary Fiction*.

OTHER BOOKS BY ROBERT WALSER
PUBLISHED BY NYRB CLASSICS

Berlin Stories
Translated and with an introduction by Susan Bernofsky

Jakob von Gunten
Translated and with an introduction by Christopher Middleton

Girlfriends, Ghosts, and Other Stories
Translated by Tom Whalen, with Nicole Köngeter and Annette Wiesner
Afterword by Tom Whalen

A Schoolboy's Diary and Other Stories
Translated by Damion Searls
Introduction by Ben Lerner

LITTLE SNOW LANDSCAPE

Stories

ROBERT WALSER

Selected and translated from the German by

TOM WHALEN

NEW YORK REVIEW BOOKS

New York

THIS IS A NEW YORK REVIEW BOOK
PUBLISHED BY THE NEW YORK REVIEW OF BOOKS
435 Hudson Street, New York, NY 10014
www.nyrb.com

Library of Congress Cataloging-in-Publication Data
Names: Walser, Robert, 1878–1956, author. | Whalen, Tom, translator, compiler.
Title: Little snow landscape and other stories / Robert Walser; selected and
    translated from the German by Tom Whalen.
Description: New York City: New York Review Books, 2021. | Series: New York
    Review books classics
Identifiers: LCCN 2020016148 (print) | LCCN 2020016149 (ebook) |
    ISBN 9781681375229 (paperback) | ISBN 9781681375236 (ebook)
Subjects: LCSH: Walser, Robert, 1878–1956—Translations into English.
Classification: LCC PT2647.A64 A2 2021 (print) | LCC PT2647.A64 (ebook) |
    DDC 833/.912—dc23
LC record available at https://lccn.loc.gov/2020016148
LC ebook record available at https://lccn.loc.gov/2020016149

ISBN 978-1-68137-522-9
Available as an electronic book; ISBN 978-1-68137-523-6

Printed in the United States of America on acid-free paper.
10 9 8 7 6 5 4 3 2 1

CONTENTS

TRANSLATOR'S NOTE

LITTLE Snow Landscape opens in 1905 with an encomium by the twenty-six-year-old Swiss author Robert Walser (1878–1956) to his *Heimat* and concludes in 1933 with a meditation on his childhood in Biel, the town of his birth, published in the last of his four years in the cantonal mental hospital in Waldau outside Bern. Between these two poles, the book maps Walser's outer and inner wanderings in various narrative modes, including essaylets, fables, idylls, tales of comedy and horror, monologues, travelogues, prose pieces both realistic and of an otherworldly artificiality. Here, you find him in the persona of a girl writing a composition on the seasons, of Don Juan at the moment he senses he's outplayed his role, of Turkey's last sultan, Abdul Hamid II, shortly after he's deposed. In "Three Stories," Walser improvises narratives on book covers of novels seen in a store window. In other pieces, young women are abused by their bosses, a man falls in love with the heroine of the penny dreadful he's reading, and the lady of a house catches her servant spread out on the divan casually reading a classic. Three longer autobiographical stories brace the whole: "Wenzel," concerning Walser's attempt in his late youth to become an actor; "Würzburg," about his walk from Munich to Würzburg in 1901 and his stay there as well as visits with a helpful friend, the German author Max Dauthendey (1867–1918); and "Louise," which takes place in the late 1890s when at nineteen, clerking in Zurich, Walser was befriended by two young Swiss roommates, Rosa Schätzle (1870–1947) and Louisa Schweizer (1869–1955), the latter the model for the story's eponymous figure, whose first name alone, even years later, "has the significance of a monument" for our narrator.

   In addition to the book as a representative offering of Walser's short prose—a form in which he was one of literature's most original, multifarious, and lucid practitioners—I kept in mind, in my selection and arrangement, the not necessarily peculiar notion of the book as, however apparently plotless, a kind of novel. For the narrator of "A Sort of Narrative"—a story very much about its own production—his sketches are chapters of a long novel he's constantly writing, a shredded or disjointed book of the self or in the first person, *zerschnittenes oder zertrenntes Ich-Buch*: I-book, self-book, first-person book, book of the ego, book of me. If in this case we take the first-person narrator (*Ich-Erzähler*) as speaking for the author, perhaps all curators of collections of Walser's sketches, stories, prose pieces, and essays (the larger and more open the umbrella the better) extract to some extent a novel of sorts, whether arranged thematically or chronologically (as here, by year of publication or composition), from Walser's vast unfinishable one.

With the exception of "The Yardstick," "The Canal," and "Children and Small Houses" from *Feuer* (Suhrkamp, 2003), a short volume edited by Bernhard Echte primarily of works rediscovered in periodicals or newspapers, the sixty-nine prose pieces herein come from the twenty-volume *Sämtliche Werke* (Suhrkamp, 1985) edited by Jochen Greven. This edition of Walser's collected novels, plays, stories, and poems contains some 3,700 pages of short prose in fourteen volumes, less than a third of which constitute the nine collections Walser published during his writing career; the uncollected short prose either appeared in journals, anthologies, and the feuilleton sections of newspapers or were unpublished works of which Walser had made fair copies. A Roman numeral following a title indicates that Walser gave the same title to more than one story. The date at the end of each piece is the year of publication or composition. Where multiple years are given (for example, "1928/29"), the exact date of the manuscript is uncertain.

To my knowledge, only three of the stories have been previously translated: "Two Little Fairy Tales," by James Kirkup in *Atlas Anthology III* (Atlas Press, 1985); "The Angel," by Susan Bernofsky and myself in *Robert Walser Rediscovered* (University Press of New England, 1985); and "Walk in the Park," by Samuel Frederick in his *Narratives Unsettled: Digression in Robert Walser, Thomas Bernhard, and Adalbert*

Stifter (Northwestern University Press, 2012). Christopher Middleton's translation of the first paragraph of "Eine Art Erzählung" ("A Sort of Narrative") also serves as the epigraph to Walser's *Selected Stories* (Farrar, Straus and Giroux, 1982).

A brief biographical note, for the sake of context, appears at the end of the book. For a fuller account, the reader is encouraged to seek out Susan Bernofsky's biography *Clairvoyant of the Small: The Life of Robert Walser*, forthcoming from Yale University Press.

For their diligence, patience, and generosity in vetting my work, I am once again grateful to Tonja Adler and Nina Joanna Bergold, as well as to Nicole Köngeter for her thorough vetting of all the texts in second draft, and to Gesche Ipsen, the book's copyeditor, and Sara Kramer and Edwin Frank of New York Review Books. Without their efforts and that of other friends and colleagues present or gone, *Little Snow Landscape* would not have been possible.

My gratitude as well to *Subtropics*, where "Rain" first appeared, and to the always thoughtful and helpful staff and management of Tarte & Törtchen on Gutbrodstrasse in Stuttgart, Germany, within whose ideal early-morning setting, over the course of more than three years, much of this book was initially translated.

—Tom Whalen
October 2020

TO MY HOME

THE SUN shines through the little hole into the little room where I am sitting and dreaming, the bells of my homeland chime. It is Sunday and on Sundays it is morning and in the morning the wind is blowing and in the wind all my cares fly away like shy birds. I feel too much the harmonious nearness of home to be able to brood over any sorrow. In the past I wept. I was so far away from my native country; so many mountains, lakes, forests, rivers, fields, and ravines lay between me and her, the beloved, the admired, the adored. This morning she embraces me and I lose myself in her voluptuous caress. No woman has such soft, such imperious arms; no woman, not even the most beautiful, such tender lips; no woman, not even the most tender, kisses with such infinite ardor as my native land kisses me. Ring, bells; play, wind; roar, forests; glow, colors—and it's all embodied in the single sweet kiss of my homeland that in this moment captivates my language, in the sweet, infinitely delicious kiss of home.

1905

TWO LITTLE FAIRY TALES

I.

IT WAS snowing in the street. Hackney cabs and cars drove up, deposited their contents, drove off again. The ladies were all stuffed into furs. The cloakroom was swarming with people. In the foyers there were greetings, exchanges of smiles and handshakes. The candles were glimmering, gowns rustling, little boots whispered and squeaked. The floor was wiped clean, and attendants were gesturing with their hands now this way, now that. The gentlemen were tied tight into their tailcoats, thus must a tailcoat fit. People were bowing. Pleasantries flew like pigeons from mouth to mouth, the women were radiant, even some of the old ones. Everyone was standing up beside their seats in order to see acquaintances, only a few were sitting down. Faces were so close to one another that the breath of one person touched the nostrils of the other standing next to him. The women's dresses were fragrant, the gentlemen's pates oily, eyes sparkled and hands said: Well, you again? Where have you been for so long? In the first row the critics sat like worshippers in a lofty church, so quietly, so devoutly. The curtain stirred a little, then the bell chimed to announce the start; whoever thought he needed to clear his throat did so hastily, and then everyone was sitting there like children in a schoolroom looking straight ahead as quiet as mice, and then something was raised and something performed.

2.

The curtain went up, everyone was curious about what would be presented, then a boy came on and began to dance. In a box in the first balcony, the queen sat surrounded by her court ladies. The dance pleased her so much she decided to go down onto the stage and say something affectionate to the boy. Soon afterward she showed up on stage; the boy looked at her with his young, beautiful eyes. He smiled. At that moment the queen, as if struck by lightning, recognized in the smile her own son and collapsed to the floor. What's wrong? asked the boy. Then she recognized the lad more and more clearly, even more so by his voice. At that, her queenly dignity was done for. She tossed her sovereignty aside and wasn't ashamed to press the youngster firmly to her heart. Her breasts rose up and down, she was weeping with joy: You are my son, she said. The audience applauded, but what was the point of applause? This woman's happiness was certainly far above all applause and would also have been able to endure hissing. Again and again, she took the head of the boy and pressed it to her heaving bosom. She kissed him, then the ladies-in-waiting arrived and reminded their mistress of the unsavoriness of the scene. At this the audience laughed, but the ladies of the court strewed their contempt on the many-headed rabble. They twitched their mouths, and then the curtain twitched and fell.

1907

LENZ'S *SOLDIERS*

I OFFER you Stolzius from Lenz's *Soldiers*. I'd like for once to see him on the stage. What an absolutely magnificent figure he is. He's so natural that one need only play him, but I'd prefer to see this figure performed by a colossus. Stolzius commits colossal stupidities; because of a girl, he poisons someone and himself; he does things that occur even today in the east of Berlin, and for exactly this reason I'd like to see the play performed. Events you can read about any old time in the newspaper are, after all, the most thrilling; the ordinary contains mysteries; in trivialities lies the supernatural. Playwrights today far too infrequently sit in coffeehouses boring their noses into the rustling evening and morning papers. Either a poet experiences something body and soul or he pilfers his subjects from the latest news, a theft that, to my knowledge, continues unpunished to this day.

Lenz's *Soldiers* is like something copied from the newspaper, with, of course, the added artistic touch, whose presence in the columns of the daily news or couriers or the daily gazettes, it's true, can seldom be observed. Still, I stake my honor on the fact that Stolzius is drawn from the newspaper, but what should I say about a woman as beautiful as Countess LaRoche? Here I'm simply stupefied, and I permit myself this stupefaction at the sight of a fully rounded female character. I imagine her as voluptuous, also that she takes tiny steps and has a bright, high-pitched voice. Naturalness and refinement surround this lady with a sweetness I would describe if it could be grasped, but, thank God, it's one of those things that elude any graspability. What this little rococo lady says surely belongs in the pot of the most beautiful literature our fatherland has to boast of in terms of language and speech. Büchner, the dramatist from the Biedermeier period, learned from

Lenz; I'm pleased it's precisely I who have been afforded the privilege to detect this.

The Countess LaRoche is powdered, but at that time females still had a knack for fusing the depths of the soul and the art of making one's toilet without one disturbing the other. It would be a little strange, perhaps, if one day this historical knowledge, too, doesn't bring me acclaim. Seriously, one should try putting a poet on stage who, like Lenz, has had the genius to give us what's natural and at the same time grand. In the play there's a charming figure of a girl, soldiers march about, barouches are driven, it's raining in a street, we see handsomely carpeted rooms on view, the landscape plays a role, and more than anything else there are gratifying characters to cast. The effect of the whole is poignant. I'm not wrong about this, for quite some time I haven't been wrong.

1907

THE WRITER (I)

IN GENERAL, the writer owns two suits, one for the street and paying visits and the other for work. He's a tidy person, sitting at his narrow writing desk has made him humble, he does without life's gay pleasures, and when he comes home after some useful outing, he quickly takes off his good suit and, as is proper, neatly hangs his pants and jacket in the wardrobe, throws on his work shirt and house shoes, goes into the kitchen, brews a cup of tea, and begins his customary labor. You see, he always drinks tea while working, it comforts him immensely and keeps him healthy, and in his opinion this makes up for all other worldly pleasures. He's not married, because he hasn't had the temerity to fall in love, since he would have to employ all the courage at his command to remain faithful to his artistic duty, which, as perhaps is known, can be quite harsh. Usually he keeps house entirely on his own, unless a girlfriend helps as he rests or an invisible guardian angel as he works. His innermost conviction tells him his life is neither particularly joyful nor dreary, neither light nor heavy, neither monotonous nor various, neither a continuous nor a frequently interrupted revelry, neither a cry nor a sustained cheerful smile; he creates, that's his life. He tries constantly to empathize with each and every thing, it is in this that his work consists, and when he stops work and stands up for a moment to roll another cigarette, take a slurp of tea, say a word to the cat, open the door to someone or glance out the window, these aren't essential interruptions, but mere artistic pauses, so to speak, or breathing exercises. Sometimes he exercises a little in his room, or it occurs to him to juggle for a bit; he also welcomes practicing singing or the declamatory art. These little things he does so as not to become a complete fool while writing, which otherwise he would easily have to fear. He is a precise person, his profession has forced this on him, for what business would slovenliness or untidiness have at his desk for days? The desire and passion for sketching life with words stems finally only from a certain precision and beautiful pedantry of the soul that suffers when it has to witness so many lovely, vibrant, urgent, transitory things flying off into the world without having been able to capture them in a notebook. What endless worries! The man with a quill in his hand is, so to speak, a hero in the half-dark, whose behavior isn't heroic and noble only because it can't be seen. One doesn't speak for nothing about "heroes of the pen." Perhaps this is just a trivial expression for an equally trivial thing, but a fireman is also somewhat insignificant, though it's definitely not out of the question that, if necessary, he can be a hero and save lives. If sometimes someone brave succeeds in rescuing a child or whatever might be in mortal danger from the rushing waters, more often than not it could be held that art and the self-sacrificing efforts of a writer can snatch from the stream of life, carelessly and heedlessly flowing past, the values of beauty on the verge of perishing and drowning, imperiling his own health, since it's not healthy to sit for ten to thirteen hours at a stretch at his novel or novella desk. He, too, can be counted among those with a valiant, plucky nature. In society, where things are always so glossy and glittering, sometimes he's aloof out of shyness, crude due to bonhomie, and clumsy from lack of polish. But dare to draw him into a conversation or weave him into the web of a friendly chat and you'll see him cast aside his awkwardness; his tongue will converse as flowingly as anyone's, his hands will take on the most natural movements, and there will be as much fire flickering in his eyes as in the eyes of any statesman, industrialist, or sailor. He's as sociable as the next person. Perhaps once in the course of an entire year he might experience nothing new because he's been laboring over a series of sentences and sounds and completing his work, but, if I may, isn't that what his imagination is for? Is imagination no longer held in esteem these days? He's capable of making a party of, let's say, about twenty people crack up laughing or quickly arouse amazement or induce tears by simply reading aloud poems of his own making. And then, when one of his books appears on the market! All the world, he imagines in his garret solitude, is rushing to it and scrambling to purchase the prettily embroidered or perhaps dark-leather copies. On the title page is his name, a circumstance which, in his ingenuous opinion, suffices to make him known throughout the whole wide round world. Then the disappointments come, the reproaches in the press, the fatal hissing, the silence right up to the grave—our man simply suffers it. He goes home, destroys all his papers, deals a terrible blow to his writing desk so that it topples over, rips apart a recently begun novel, shreds his writing pad, throws his supply of pens out the window, and writes to his publisher, "Dear Sir, I beg you to stop believing in me," and sails off on his peregrinations. After a short time, incidentally, his wrath and shame strike him as ridiculous, and he tells himself it's his duty and obligation to resume work. Or so one writer does it, another might do it a degree differently. Never does a born writer lose courage; he has an almost unbroken confidence in the world and the thousands of new possibilities it affords him each and every day. He knows every kind of despair, but also every kind of happiness. The odd thing is that it's the successes rather than the failures that make him doubt himself. This, however, perhaps only occurs because his cognition machine is in constant motion. Now and then a writer makes a bundle, but he's almost embarrassed to have acquired heaps of money, and in cases such as these he deliberately belittles himself in order to dodge, if at all possible, the poisoned arrows of envy and ridicule. That's a completely natural response. But what if he exists poor and despised in damp, cold rooms, at tables over whose plates vermin crawl, in straw beds, in houses full of a repulsive racket and clamor, on totally desolate roads, in the wetness of the rain pouring down, in search of a means of subsistence—which, perhaps because he cuts a stupid figure, no rational man would grant him—under the glare of the big-city sun, in lodgings full of adversity, in regions filled with storms, or in asylums without the kindness and sense of home so nicely embodied in the word? Do you think such misfortune is out of the question? Now then: the writer can also experience danger, and how he handles this will depend on his genius at reconciling himself to every horrid circumstance. The writer loves the world, because if he can no longer love it he feels he stops being a child. Anyway, in this particular case he's mostly just a mediocre writer, he distinctly senses this, and so avoids presenting a disgruntled face to life. Thus, quite often it happens that he's also seen as an undiscerning, imbecilic dreamer, which disregards the fact that he's a human being who doesn't let himself indulge in ridicule or hatred, as these feelings would all too easily rob him of the desire to create.

1907

WENZEL

IT'S THE evening of New Year's Day and we find ourselves in the City Theater in Twann, a little town founded by the Romans which lies at the foot of a high mountain range. However, we wish not to discourse on geography but instead watch Schiller's *Robbers*, since this is what usually opens the season in Twann. The play is performed with fervor—at least Wenzel, a young, approximately seventeen-year-old apprentice in a wireworks factory, thinks this. He stands or sits above in the gallery whose collapse, as is generally known, is an imminent threat. The president of the municipal council pays a visit with his walking stick to the gallery bridge, gives it his swift and concise attention, then goes down to his box below, the swinging suspended bridge assessed as still strong enough to hold for tonight.

How splendidly thrilling this *Robbers* is and how full the theater! Something green is seen on the stage; this is Amalia's garden; a flashing sword has been drawn, and Franz, a skinny-legged villain, has turned tail, that's to say, is fleeing from the woman in black. A hundred times beautiful were the words: "Kings are beggars, beggars kings!" Wenzel shivered.

Then there is a night scene with a whiff of the Middle Ages: pursued by ghostly fears, Franz steps outside in a nightshirt. And as he conducts himself in the manner prescribed by the author, throwing himself on the ground and delivering prodigious words, a maker of watchcases bellows from the gallery: *"Il est fou!"* Thereupon a riot ensues. The drunken New Year's reveler is hauled down and thrown out, three others throw themselves on him, which of course produces stamping and cursing, and from below the actor playing Franz flings a haughty, smoldering look at the scene above. "How little understanding the world has for high art," muses Wenzel.

From then on, his secret resolve is made: he wants to become an actor. As a result, he betakes himself to the Rüfenach bookstore in Neuquartierstrasse to purchase the classics. He spends money, indeed quite a bit, admittedly a scarce resource for an apprentice, but what wouldn't one do for this first enthusiasm roiling inside him! And so he lugs Schiller, Goethe, and the great Englishman under his arm up to his attic room in his family's home and begins to study the roles.

He also reads tantalizing biographies of great stage artists in periodicals like *The Garden Arbor*, *From Rock to Ocean*, and *The Book for Everyone*. It seems as though these yet-to-be-famous also once lacked talent, just like Wenzel, who for the time being hasn't any, and who is just as shy as those great ones, poor just like them, and who also has parents who don't understand him, just as they had! But the ones destined to be famous set out early in search of a patron. At the moment Wenzel wishes to do precisely that.

In Twann lives a rich gentleman, a banker by trade and heritage, a kind of dandy who rides through the streets of the town on horseback in his precious suit. A kind of prince, of whom it's known that he loves the arts and is generous. Every year on the night of St. Nicholas this gentleman throws coins to needy schoolchildren. Well, perhaps a struggling indigent, someone imbued with artistic aspirations, will suit him as much as the deprived youngsters. Art is also a kind of hunger, and hunger for art afflicts you no less than actual thirst and hunger.

Wenzel drafts the following letter:

Most honored Sir,

I dare to make a request. I wish to become an actor and think I will need proficient training. I need to learn how to speak and conduct myself. This costs money. Would you advance me something for this? A great deal is said about your kindness and benevolence. I am employed in wiredrawing, and if you would like to inquire about my humble person—but why do that? I ask you please not to think I am begging. The sincerity of my soul prompts me to write and earnestly ask this of you, it cannot beg. A thousand francs would suffice. I can bear privation. My love of art is boundless, I don't know how large it is, but I don't measure it, I suffer from it, so it must be immense. My reading of the classics has given me courage. Forgive me for believing you might be willing to provide me with money. I apologize for the audacity of this soul that thinks there are people eager to help. Don't take offense at my tone, it's the same one the young Schiller spoke in.

Respectfully and hopefully,
Wenzel

The letter is posted. Meanwhile roles are memorized. The cheerful, courageous youngster dresses himself in a velvet vest his father used to wear at weddings. Over his shoulder he flings an old coat of his uncle's, who had haggled over it in a town along the Mississippi, and he winds a silk sash around his hips. His head receives an appropriate covering, a pan made out of felt adorned with a wild duck's feather. The hand knew to procure a grayish pistol, and on the legs adhere ranger boots. Thus fitted out, he rehearses the part of Karl Moor, Schiller's robber.

Meanwhile, from the villa of the prince of the arts, the answer is already winging back:

Dear young friend, beware of a career on the stage, it's treacherous. Believe me that I want the best for you when I attempt to prevent you from crossing into the world of grand words, beautiful gestures, and glittering costumes. You have been seduced by appearances. Remain an industrious and humble citizen and by all means read the classics, but calmly and without taking the contents of these beautiful books more seriously than is salutary and sensible.

Salutary and sensible. These are no words to comfort or calm a fervid artistic heart. Wenzel pays the director of Twann's City Theater a visit to ask if he'll take him with him on the tour. He could also haul boxes or hand out fliers. He would have said he could in fact probably clean shoes, but he didn't have the courage to let this escape from his lips. Spanish Mustache answered him: "Young man, I can't possibly take on that responsibility."

There are many eighteen-year-olds in the world, some willing to heed advice, others who won't listen to anything. Wenzel wants to have his way. He writes: "Noble Sir and Master," and under this title addresses a letter to a metropolitan, almost entirely great actor. From this an audition ensues. A couple of dusty laurel wreaths hear the performance, a woman who wonderfully reminds us of northern Germany and novels from *The Garden Arbor*, and the man himself, the thunderously handsome actor standing there with a face that reminds Wenzel of a portraiture. This visit ends woefully.

At home, Wenzel practices doing his makeup and attempts to play Hamlet in his attic room. Ferdinand in Schiller's *Love and Intrigue* goes smoothly. The mirror serves to examine one's ability to confer on the face various features and characters. Often his hair is flung about, since this is more picturesque and feigns a touch of casualness. Wenzel also ties self-cut snippets of silk around his collar, which suits him well and seems to transport him a hundred years back in time. Mountains are ascended; lovely circular pastures gracefully formed by Nature must serve as the stage. Fir trees are all around and heaven above, and in the middle stands the budding, blushing actor Wenzel. One day he joins Twann's Drama Society.

A professor of literature and editor of the *Express* leads the enterprise. Wenzel finds him dry and arrogant. The exercises are held in a brightly lit assembly hall, and the professor corrects their elocution. A heroine named Fräulein Sturm is also present, and a comical old woman, twenty years old and with a turned-up nose, called Fräulein Knuchel. She, too, might have preferred to have taken up the tragic line, but her suffering was laughed at and she was tossed into comedy. Wenzel is given *Niklaus Leuenberger*, a historical tragedy, to transcribe. He takes the manuscript home.

After supper one evening his father wants to fling the thing into the fire. Wenzel defends the manuscript; not unlike a lion, he covers it with his protecting hand and shouts: "Are you a barbarian, Father, that you want to tear to bits the works of acknowledged poets and toss them into the furnace? What have these poor beautiful pages ever done to harm you? Better to give me a thrashing if you're irate about a pursuit that you, it appears, don't appreciate and are only able to abhor! Do you think you can turn me against my plans by committing an act of anger and imprudence? What do you want? Slap me in the face but don't lay a hand on this literary work whose well-established fame is an inviolability. Not only that, I'm earning money by transcribing this manuscript. How can you be so enraged about a piece of innocent dramatic poetry that you crave to destroy it? You would do better to beat the ideas out of my head where they roil, but how is that possible without breaking my head? Father, you know I've wanted and to this day still want to become an actor. What good is fatherly affection to me if it can't do anything but hate and strive to eradicate what's dearest and the most important thing in the world to me? How can I ever be cured from the fever that has gripped me by such, as it were, inappropriate remedies as you allow yourself to employ, and how is it imaginable that a love of art is only a fever? And even if it is! Your assaults can never convince me of the harmfulness of this malady, because in order to do so you would have to confront me much more dispassionately. Fervor against fervor, sickness against sickness! Yes, the vehemence with which you seek to smother with your hands and fists the higher learning I'm devoted to and which bothers you so much I permit myself to call a kind of fanaticism, a violence. If what enflames me so much is nonsense, well, then one day it will present its true form and voice and I'll give up all thoughts of art and be miserable. Your behavior, dear Father, doesn't make me unhappy but angry, and now allow me to leave the room and site of this unkind scene and go to my garret." Thus ended a fierce assault on a dramatic manuscript.

Another scene that takes place shortly thereafter turns out much gentler, albeit much more painful. The setting is the kitchen. Wenzel is helping his sister Mathilde dry the dishes. She says: "Oh Wenzel, I don't really believe in your talent. Just think of the elegant young lover von Müller. My god, compared to him you're a crude, common little weed. What manners you have. Do you believe that with the little bit of enthusiasm you possess you can step onto the world of the stage? Look at yourself. Or do you think you can survive in the big world with your few parts in *Mary Stuart* or as Mortimer or whatever the gentleman is called you're always declaiming in your shoe polish? I can't really fathom it. Have you ever worn gloves? You're still far, far too self-conscious for that. You're too shy even to open your mouth around my girlfriends, how much less will you be able to do that on stage in front of the eyes of the world gathered there. For others that may be the easiest thing there is, but for you it's difficult, believe me. You'd be better off writing poetry."

Wenzel replies: "I know quite well how immature and awkward I am, but I believe art doesn't only depend on cockiness. What kind of artists are they, your youthful and oldish gentleman-lovers of whom you speak, those von Becks and von Müllers and von Almens. What they can do I'll soon be able to do easily as well. Of course, they possess a splendid appearance and are insolent like nothing else. I could try for ages to follow them in that before I could ever even catch up, much less surpass them. That's certainly regrettable. But if you expect me to write poems instead of sticking to the beauty of acting, I for my part must thank you."

The Drama Society is putting on a farce by Schönthan. Wenzel is to play a prince's lackey who, among other things, has to take a slap in the face. No, that he cannot play, that's too deplorable. That's too injurious. On the afternoon of the performance he flees into the mountains. The wild, cold wind roars in, the tall firs bend and bow down, how good and natural this is in comparison to a lackey awaiting a smack in the face. He absents himself from the performance, it's too stupid, too crushing, too miserable, he can't do it. "Do I have that deep a love for the stage?" Wenzel thinks. "Is that love?" The role isn't good enough for him; he asks himself if that's proof he's incapable of performing on stage. His conscience tells him: "Love and ardor endure everything, even a slap in the face."

When two months have elapsed Wenzel finds himself in a distant large city earning his living at a shipping company; he receives a salary, he saves, he takes proper lessons with a recognized, proficient leading actor. Now surely this should finally get things moving. He performs lung, tongue, lip, and breathing exercises and learns how to enunciate the vowels and consonants correctly and clearly. He's impressed by how methodically the lessons move forward, and the actor tells him: "You're making progress." At this moment the teacher and mentor receives the following letter from Wenzel's father:

To the actor Jank:

You are giving lessons to my son. This news, to my great dismay, came to me through relatives there with whom Wenzel, the utter ingrate, seems to be taking his room and board. You are not to do this. You should desist from this immediately. I've suffered my fair share of these intolerable episodes of my son's. It's sad that you, with whom the rascal has had the dexterity to ingratiate himself, didn't send him away immediately, but have instead, as I've learned, supported him in his belief and predilection for things that, in my eyes and those of people who also lead respectable lives, have always been seen as indecent. The last thing I need is for my son, the offspring of good, honest parents, to join traveling players and count himself one of those who regard the shame in which they dissolutely sprawl and live as something proper and permissible. I can imagine that you welcome the extra earnings from your teaching, but the lesson that you and those of your disposition and milieu teach causes harm, is sinful, and perniciously affects one's morality and character. Who you are I don't know, it's sufficient that I feel you're one of those people who has no position in society, whose conduct is untrustworthy and whose way of life is deeply deranged. I have indicated to which class of people I assume you belong. Wenzel is a good-for-nothing and would deserve to be left to the likes of you. Perhaps you still have a last bit of honor, Mr. Actor and Stage Comedian, for these words to cause you to toss the lout down the stairs, or else assistance from the police will be at my immediate disposal.

Respectfully,
Wenzel's father

With that the blessed lessons end. The one who plays heroic parts tells Wenzel: "Look, your father is really something. I could sue him if I wanted to, but I won't. His insults don't affect me and let's leave it at that. What he thinks of us artists are the ideas of a narrow-minded bourgeois, and I wonder which of us is the better and more benevolent citizen, me or your father."

Wenzel goes home to his aunts, with whom he lives, and reproaches them. He says: "What business is it of yours to interfere with my artistic aims and goals? Well? You do understand that now I'll be moving? The wonderful crêpes with preserves I've eaten here are not worth my having to quietly suffer seeing my connections to such a splendid person as this fine actor being undone and severed. For all I care, eat the crêpes yourselves. I'm old enough to dine in restaurants and live where I please. I'll move out on the first. And I'll definitely not be staying in this town much longer. I've had enough of it."

In fact, Wenzel soon departs. He packs his thoughts of acting into his small suitcase, not forgetting the classics. He travels to Swabia. One day, however, he is told there, quite honestly and in simple terms: "Young man, wherever you come from, whether you are of respectable or not so respectable bourgeois descent, you lack the divine spark."

1909

FAREWELL

I ALWAYS did as I liked.* Whenever something occurred to me, I rang the bell and was brought what I desired. I smoked a pipe, and if it didn't allow for a proper draw, the head of one of my slaves leapt off his obsequious shoulders. My life was like a dream, and I believe, when I consider the thing now, that I most definitely resembled a potentate. Often I rode out surrounded by countless attendants. Obviously, I governed poorly, I didn't care about taking great pains in this regard, for which, in fact, they've now run me off. Governed? I would smile apathetically—this is how I envisioned governing. Whenever I was sprawling on the billowy sofa, someone would approach me, that is, he would crawl on all fours and say something. I called this taking care of state business.

I've never been keen on politics, that is, I followed the movements of my female dancers, that was the politics I pursued. Of course, I am notorious throughout the world as princely vermin. Well then, cleanse the country now, if you can, but watch out that the Orient doesn't die under your hands doing the cleaning. Actually, you were perfectly right to depose me, since, in any case, I would have tyrannized you as you exercised your duties, by being perfectly, imperially indifferent. It's also alleged that I've committed murder. But let's not talk about that. Supposedly much has been written against me in the European newspapers; I, however, have never taken up a newspaper, much less troubled my august eyes to read one. Poor Orient, ah, now they're killing you. I was

---

*"Farewell" is narrated by Abdul Hamid II, Turkey's last sultan, who was dethroned in 1909, the year the story appeared in the *Neue Rundschau*.

only a little murderer, I killed my creatures; they, however, have killed half the earth. For what will we become, now that they've civilized us?

In Turkey, whose anointed leader I was, there had never been capable people, but now there are. Our gardens will wither, our mosques will soon be superfluous, our prophets will be derided.

I lounged about in my chambers and resembled an inviolable God. I never worked and was even too sleepy to give commands. I commanded with my eyes, and those around me understood this language. Often, I would give commands with my large Turkish nose, and when I sneezed the provinces were ravaged by my hordes. To them I was the blazing and darkening of the sun, but now they are no longer in need of this. There is neither grace nor disgrace under the Crescent. Only now do I fully realize how strange my life as a sovereign was. When my head or something else itched, unrest arose in the palace and a trembling spread through my kingdom like the tremors of an angry earthquake. Yes, I, I still ruled. Then followed tedious, tepid Japan with its military successes. Ah, yes, that's the last thing we needed. Now we're being Japanized or Europeanized, it's all the same. Oh, it was so strange. The truth of the matter, you should know, is that I did not rule at all, I just sat there and puffed smoke from my pipe. I relinquished the office of governance to my factotums. Perhaps that was a mistake, but I shall forbid myself to engage in any speculations. One day someone thought I should be informed that Paris is a beautiful city. I had the one who said that baked and fried, and the poor wretch smiled. They smiled when I had them tortured. They believed in me, and then they began to no longer believe in anything; therefore I believe it will become boring to be in Turkey.

Now I can go to Paris and live in the Grand Hotel for a thousand francs a day. And that will be unspeakably droll and equally unspeakably vapid. Was I dreaming? Often, I strolled under the snow of blossoming trees. A fountain splashed not far away. I was always sick with desire and longing. Those who dared to look me directly in the face I had poisoned. Then I whistled and my wives appeared, and I didn't know if I should have them bled to death before my eyes or if it would be nicer to embrace their trembling limbs. Their arms! My eyes now always teem with arms, legs, bangles, lips, robes, and the movements of dancing women. The women, the most beautiful and most voluptuous, it pleased me, from time to time, to leave standing there timidly before me, simply to behold and refuse them. I had already become totally insane with lechery.

And meanwhile, asses that they are, they wrote articles against me. The blinkered, the deluded! But it seems all this had to come to pass. Allah is against us. Islam is over with. Through the desert, where the sound of my name compelled respect from the hyenas, trains will travel. Turks will don hats and look like Germans. We will be forced to go into business, and if we're unable to do that, we will simply be shot. In general, I think I was at least something of a personality on the throne. All right, I overindulged on the throne! Where does that happen today? Kings have to clean up the state, otherwise they will be dethroned. I was the last sovereign still living in a real palace. My successors will reside only in a government building.

1909

ILLUSION

R EGARDLESS, I at least had a map, it hung on the wall in my study, and there I could travel with the tip of my nose or fingertips as much as I desired out into the wide world. Vast, sweeping Russia as a body alone enraptured me. Amidst this mighty corpus, exactly at the fixed, beautiful, true midpoint of a center, lay, silvered in snowflakes, the city of Moscow. Sleighs, minute and delicate, drawn through the strange streets by sprightly horses, flew past over the snow. As it grew dark, lights from windows of the princely palaces shone splendidly, and it was glorious to see how, from some of the windows, the sweet and beautiful shapes of women seemed to be leaning forward. Songs rang forth, ancient Russian songs enchanted by the national melancholy, beguiling me. I stepped into a house of pleasure, and there I could look into their eyes, the eyes of the proud Russian women. They smiled, but with inexpressible contempt, as if they loved this life and at the same time despised it. Wonderful dances were performed, ethereal, beautiful paintings adorned the walls of the halls from top to bottom. I beheld almost nothing ignoble, either because my eyes were overflowing with visible and invisible delights or because I was inspirited with the predilection to find everything beautiful. I sat down at one of the sumptuously laid tables and impatiently awaited what would come. Wines were served to me by tall men wearing caps; then, convinced by the modesty I was radiating, favored as I was, a woman, a lady from head to toe, advanced toward me and with a nice, inexpressibly graceful bow sat down at the table next to me and commanded me, in the language every lover understands, to pour her a glass of wine. She sipped from the glass like a squirrel. In the course of our conversation—oddly, I could suddenly understand Russian well—I asked her if she would give me her hand to kiss. She allowed this and ripples of bliss came over me as I was permitted to press my lips upon this pale, sweet, pure-as-snow, white wonder; it seemed to me as if by this touch and movement I were drinking in a new belief in God, to which I surrendered with all the power and pleasure of my soul. She smiled and called me a nice man. And then, and then, oh miserable me, everything vanished, and again I was sitting in my pensive writing room. New ideas poured into me, it seemed as if I had to roll away boulders. Already it was after midnight; befuddled by fancy, I stepped to the open, cold window and gave myself up to the sight of the overwhelming stillness.

1910

BÜCHNER'S FLIGHT

On a certain covert night, shot through by the odious and dreadful fear of being arrested by police henchmen, Georg Büchner, the youthful star flashing brightly in the firmament of German poetry, slipped away from the brutality, stupidity, and violence of political skulduggery. In the anxious urgency animating him to be off at once, he stuck the manuscript of *Danton's Death* in the pocket of his ample, audaciously cut student coat, from which it whitely flashed. Through his soul *Sturm und Drang* surged like a wide, majestic river; a never before known nor suspected joy seized his being, as he quickly and with huge strides proceeded down the moonlit country road and saw, lying open before him, the broad expanse of land that midnight embraced in its generous, voluptuous arms. Germany lay sensually and naturally before him, and instinctively some old, beautiful folk songs occurred to the noble youth, and he loudly sang their lyrics and music like an unabashed, merry itinerant tailor or cobbler embarked on his nocturnal trek. From time to time, with his slender, elegant hand, he gripped in his pocket the dramatic, not-yet-famous work of art to make sure it was still there. And it was, and a joyful force brimming over with desire seized and rippled through him, knowing that he was free just when he was supposed to be walking into a tyrant's dungeon. Many times, huge, black, ferociously riven clouds occluded the moon, as if wanting to incarcerate or strangle it, but it always reemerged from the surrounding darkness to nobility and freedom, like a beautiful child with inquisitive eyes casting its rays over the silent world. Büchner could have dropped to his knees and prayed to God in thanks for the sheer, wild, sweet pleasure of his escape, but he put this out of his mind and ran as fast as he could, behind him the enormity experienced, before him the unknown, unexperienced enormity still to come. So he ran on and the wind blew in his beautiful face.

1912

CINEMA

COUNT and Countess are sitting at breakfast. In the doorway, the servant appears and hands over to his gracious master an apparently important letter, which the count opens and reads.

The letter's contents: "Dear, or if you would prefer, nobly born, inadequately exalted, kind sir, listen, an inheritance has fallen to you of around two hundred thousand marks. Be astonished and happy. You may take receipt of the money in person as soon as you wish."

The count apprises his wife of the good fortune that has dropped into his lap, and the countess, who bears some resemblance to a waitress, embraces the highly improbable count. The two people remove themselves, leaving the letter, however, lying on the table. The valet comes and, in a fiendish pantomime, reads it. He knows what he has to do, the scoundrel.

Now, "Ladies and Gentlemen, get your beer, sausage sandwiches, chocolate, pretzels, oranges!" shouts the usher during the intermission.

The count and the valet, the perfidious monster that bit by bit he reveals himself to be, have betaken themselves onto an ocean liner and are now in the cabin. The servant pulls his master's boots off, and the latter lies down to sleep. How careless this is shall become evident at once, since now the villain shows himself to be a murderous valet pouring a mind-filching liquid into the mouth he forcefully pries open. In an instant the master's hands and feet are bound, and the next moment the robber has snatched up the letter with the money, the poor gentleman is tossed into the trunk, and the lid slammed shut.

"Get your beer, soda pop, nut rolls, sandwiches, and chocolate, Ladies and Gentlemen!" shouts the ogre once again. Some of the provincial gentry consent to a little refreshment.

Now the traitorous servant prances about in the suits of the violated count languishing in the trunk bound for America. He appears demonic, the unparalleled villain.

More images reel past. Finally, it all ends well. The servant is seized by the fists of a detective, and with his two hundred thousand marks the count, albeit improbably, happily returns home.

Now a piano piece follows, with a renewed "Get your beer, Ladies and Gentlemen!"

1912

BIRCH-PFEIFFER

I VENTURE to guess if ever someone possessed talent it was the famous Birch-Pfeiffer. She lived in idyllic Zurich and called herself Countess. Corpulent and at the same time slender of figure, she had an impressive, yes, one can say bewitching and charming appearance. Everyone paid homage to her, everyone and everything knelt down before her. She achieved the most profuse success, as a person and as a writer. Gathering her broad skirts, she swung herself up onto the stage with a magnificent bound, and from then on she dominated it. She was one of the exceptionally gifted, and she herself bestowed grace, pleasure, and delight in abundance. Even today, after so many years, her bonbons, that is, her plays, are performed. She wrote so sweetly and lovingly that all those who rushed to the theater to watch her plays had to weep from emotional and spiritual anguish. She had tossed the melodrama, which was a hit, under the nose of a love-thirsty world, and the stirred-and-shaken world thanked her and lifted her up on its shoulders and paraded her around in triumph. One of her most frequently performed plays is *Village and City*, a work in five acts. While a Büchner, who lived at the same time as Birch-Pfeiffer, remained as good as lost and unrecognized, they screamed for her, and when she appeared in front of the curtain, broad and tall as she was, there was no end to the adulation. Let us allow ourselves to present a few peculiarities about the great woman: oh, that we might die of memories of this incomparable and unforgettable female. The sweetie, she had such a strong bosom that whoever set eyes on her fell as if struck by a cannonball. Thusly she stormed about like a mobile hectoliter barrel, and no one could look at her eagle's beak without being greatly affected by the noble sight. She was fond of wearing, as it says in the annals, garish yellow stockings with crispy black garters. Her waist was mighty, and from behind her back heaved up like a mountain, as though it were about to burst. Her stormy-dark eyes always glared punitively, and her mouth was clenched tight. Those are some of her most distinctive features. There's still more left for us to say but instead let us remain silent and ... revere her!

1912

LENZ

Sesenheim. Drawing room.

FRIEDERIKA: Why are you sad, dear Herr Lenz? Try to appear more cheerful. Look how happy I am. Can I help it that I'm in a good mood? Does it offend you? Does it offend you that I don't want to be gloomy and ill-tempered? How beautiful the world seems even today! Don't you think so as well?

LENZ: I can't bear it any longer. I've got to get out. Quick. You're happy, you're heavenly, and I'm all the more miserable for that. When I see you so beautiful, I have to hold your head in my hands and kiss you, and you don't want this, you won't ever want this, never desire it. We aren't meant for one another. I'm not meant for anything in this world.

FRIEDERIKA:. Why lose all your courage like this? You can be so hurtful. You could give me real pleasure if only you wanted to feel a little better, but you don't want to.

LENZ: I'm incapable of it.

FRIEDERIKA: Then go. Leave. Let me alone. That's for the best.

LENZ: Don't you know how much I love you? How I worship you?

FRIEDERIKA: That wasn't necessary for you to say. Here comes Goethe. God knows I'm seized, torn apart, when I see this dear man.

Friederika's chamber. Dawn.

LENZ: Quietly, quietly. So that no one at all might see me. How disgusting I am! But it's better to be disgusting and hideous than so hopeless. Can't a miserable wretch be happy, too? Why must one person be granted nothing, not a thing, and another everything that is beautiful? Better to be depraved than a nothing. O Nature, how divine you are! Even upon the souls of those who deface you, you cast joy and bliss. Ah, here are her stockings. *(Kisses them.)* I'm mad. Look how I tremble, like a criminal. How holy these things are. How they assail me. If someone were to come in—be off!—I'd be ruined forever.

Strasbourg. On top of the Münster Cathedral.

GOETHE: How magnificent the view is! Never have reflection and pleasure been better united than in this majestic place. When one indulges the desire to allow the eye to rove ever farther, the beautiful panorama grows more and more instructive. How the river shimmers there in the wide, benevolent land. Like a legend, like an old, good saying it winds through the vast plain. There in the distance stand the mountains. One can see everything at once and still never tire of looking at it. The eye is a strange apparatus. It seizes everything and releases it again. Down there in the old, charming alleys: how dreamily the people tread and walk and go about their day's work. From up here, one can see well how beneficent and honest we are, affected by our healthy daily habits. Isn't order always beauty?

LENZ: The storm must roar into our German literature and make the old dilapidated house shudder in its beams, its walls, its joints. If only the lads would speak frankly for once. My *Tutor* should chase them into a bit of terror. Yes, hound them, take them by storm. We must climb. We must take risks. In nature it's like in the rushing and whispering of blood. Literature, our beautiful literature, must get some blood into its pale, old, ashen cheeks. Beautiful? Beautiful can only be what surges, refreshes. Ah, I want to take hammers and hammer straight on. The spark, Goethe, the spark. I believe my *Soldiers* has to become like a lightning bolt that ignites it.

GOETHE *looks at him, smiles.*

Alley. It's raining.

LENZ: Everything is becoming so barbaric here. I'm going to ruin. No warning signs. The illusions disappear. No more dreams. And how dead, how sultry everything is. Does it really have to rain now? To what end is there rain? The rain is there so that the world can have umbrellas and wet streets. Behind my eyes it's boiling hot. What I want most now is to crawl. This eternal walking! What stupid troubles we make for ourselves . . .

Weimar. Castle hall.

DUCHESS: So, this is what you look like? Don't be afraid to come closer. Since you are welcomed here, you are allowed to feel confident. Your dramatic works resemble you. There's something shy and savage in both you and your writing. Put both aside a little, so that you can take more pleasure in yourself and your poetic passion. I'm truly delighted you felt inclined to come to us and hope it will soon be to your liking. Life desires a certain cozy warmth and proper breadth. But I'm acting like I intend to lecture you. I want to and I shouldn't; I should be only too pleased that you are here, and I am, believe me. Have you found affordable lodgings yet? Yes? That's good. Surely our Weimar can become home to you, it has much to offer. You only have to know how to take it and enjoy it as it is. Seeing you like this, one believes one might feel entitled to give you a little schooling. Do you resent my speaking so affectionately to you? No? All the better. But I'm prattling, and the duke awaits me.

LENZ *blushing; very insecure, wants to say something.*

DUCHESS: Ah, there's no need for special expressions of gratitude. Extend them to me some other time. Or better, not at all. I like your face. That's enough. It has already expressed every courtesy and politeness. I shall see to it that we meet again. (*Exits.*)

LENZ: Am I floating? Where am I?

Terrace. View of the park.

LENZ: I write and create nothing. This eternal curtseying and ingratiating oneself. This coldness, these pointless formalities. Am I still a human being? Why am I disappointed? Why is there nowhere I want to snuggle up to in the world? Strasbourg was quite different. Was it perhaps better there? I don't know. Can I settle down nowhere? Is there nowhere for me to hold my own? I'm terrified. I feel ghastly.

Night. In the room of Countess So-and-So, lady-in-waiting.

COUNTESS: What's the meaning of this?

LENZ: Let me be, let me be. Grant me the pleasure of lying at your feet. How beautiful, how comforting this moment is for this horribly tormented soul dying of thirst. Oh, don't ring the bell, don't summon your servants. Am I a robber, a burglar? I admit I tore in unannounced. When one is in love, should one first have to care at length for the usual conventions? How beautiful you are, and how happy I am, and how fervently, how sincerely I want not to displease you. Can words that come from the heart of a man who worships you offend you? Surely that's possible, surely, surely. For me to offend you, to upset you with even so much as a breath? How could that be possible? Don't look at me, don't look at me so cruelly. Your eyes which are so beautiful don't deserve to have to look so coldly, so unfriendly, so unkindly. Save me. I'm perdition-bound if you have no feeling for me. Have you no feeling? Are you not allowed to have any? Am I now smashed to bits? Am I lost along with all my heavenly, beautiful dreams? Do you know how sweetly, how beautifully I dreamed? But I no longer know what to say. I should be quiet, I should realize in fact that I've committed the greatest of all indecencies, I should feel that everything is cold and has come to an end.

COUNTESS: I'm speechless.

LENZ: How beautiful you are. This bosom, these arms, that body. Can so much loveliness behave other than gently?

COUNTESS: Remove yourself at once! I need not tell you that you've demonstrated how desperate and impossible you are. Have you lost all good sense? I have to think so.

The Duke's study.

GOETHE: He's an ass.

DUKE: An unfortunate child. Otherwise what he has done would be inconceivable. He should be taken away in a gentle fashion. My court cannot suffer such things.

1912

THE HERMITAGE

SOMEWHERE in Switzerland, in the mountain region, pinched between rocks and surrounded by a fir forest, is the retreat of a recluse. It's so beautiful that when you behold it you can't believe it's real, find it instead the tender, dreamy fantasy of a poet. As if it sprang from a lovely poem you can only sense, perceive, feel, and sing, the peaceful little cottage, hemmed by a garden, sits and lies and stands there with a cross in front of it, enveloped by all the lovely, sweet scents of a devotion inexpressible in words. Hopefully the lovely little structure is still standing today. I saw it a few years ago, and I would have to weep at the thought that it might have disappeared, which I don't want to think possible. A hermit resides there. One cannot exist more beautifully, more refinedly and better. The house he inhabits resembles a picture, and so does the life he lives. Wordlessly and free from outside influence he lives his day therein. In the hermit's hut, day and night are like brother and sister. The week flows there like a quiet, small, deep stream, the months know and greet and love one another like old, dear friends, and the year is a long and brief dream. Oh, how enviable, how fine, how rich is this lonely man's life, who performs his prayers and healthy daily tasks equally beautifully and calmly. When he awakens early in the morning, the holy and happy concert that the forest birds, unsolicited, begin to sing trills into his ears, and the first sweet sunbeams frisk about his room. Enchanted man. He's perfectly entitled to his deliberate pace, and wherever his eyes might wander he is surrounded by nature. A millionaire with his immense expenditures seems like a beggar compared to the inhabitant of this sweetness and secrecy. Every movement here is a thought and every act enveloped by sublimity; but the recluse doesn't need to think about anything, because the one to whom he prays thinks for him. Like the sons of kings mysteriously and gracefully approaching from afar, evening comes on to give the dear day a kiss and put it to sleep, followed by nights of mists and stars and wondrous darkness. How happily would I be the hermit and dwell in the hermitage.

1913

DREAM VISION

I SAW SOMETHING sweet, something mischievous, comical, capricious, yet also not so capricious that it couldn't make on me and many others a deep impression. The seriousness of life rang like a bell into the licentious whispering and jingling and murmuring all around. The leaves whispered; the sweet, soft night wind blew; laughter resounded; tears flowed from eyes open wide; hearts trembled among all the magical impressions; music enframed and engulfed and engoldened the entirety. It was wonderful how the dear, beautiful, thousand-year-old melodies penetrated my heart, like in a fairy tale whose beautiful contents children happily believe in. As I saw what I saw I became a child, and the whole world, for as far as I could see, seemed reborn, much like I and others felt who also saw it. Ribbons red, green, and blue wreathed like graceful, harmless snakes, twining through the gentle tumult of life. Life was calm and wild at the same time, with a scent of, oh, such unspeakable happiness, and in the blink of an eye the benevolent, innocent joy of love lay in tatters on the ground. There was no one who didn't love and covet. Everybody was pulled into beautiful currents of silver and fire, and all of them desired this. Anguish and joy, pain and pleasure, reflected glowingly and thirstily in the eyes of all those who watched everyone taking part in the game. Some eyes were lowered, and there were lips that grew pale and stammered. Voluptuous roses, melting into their own colors, shone forth enticingly and bewitchingly from the opulent image. Lights flickered and flirted from behind a dark, phantasmagoric green, like mysterious eyes beneath eyebrows; waves flowed over smooth rocks; hope and longing set the tone in this place. Now the area was what it was, then once again it was a thought, so delicate that the one who thought it had to fear losing it. Aren't lost thoughts always the most beautiful? What we have we don't cherish, and what we possess is devalued. Oh, how lovely the lake was in the near distance, silvered by the moon which, falling in love with the water, plunged glowingly into the lake to be blissfully reflected in the body it adored. The water shuddered and lay completely still, delighted by the adoration. Moon and water were like boyfriend and girlfriend captivated by a kiss to which they surrendered. Soon everything melted and faded away, then I saw it emerge again from the obscurity, only this time more richly endowed. Silently, now purely eyes, I sat there and was oblivious of all reality.

1913

THE DRESSMAKER

IN AN OLD, if not quite ancient house in the Obergasse, there lived, as I was told, a young pretty woman, her purpose and profession in life that of a dressmaker. She resided in a large, hall-like apartment that in our opinion would have been more suitable as a meeting place for scholars, city councilors, and the like than as living space for a fun-loving and fine-boned woman. At night the youthful fashion designer could hardly get to sleep in her bed. Reader, what about you? Would you want to live in such a horrid, sad old chamber? Surely you as well would have found no real rest there. The room was so huge, the silence that prevailed in this chamber so odd and the darkness so thick, mysterious, and unfathomable. You could have stuck your finger into it, like into a kind of thick black milk, so densely dark was the sinister room. As though abandoned by the entire civilized and sophisticated world, the beautiful woman lay in the long, equivocal, dark nights, feeling so helpless and unprotected, constantly under the impression that something horrible, terrifying, and monstrous would happen. Her room seemed to her like a tomb, and when she climbed into bed, her fearful imagination whispered in her ear that she was climbing into a coffin. One night, in the deadly quiet, inexpressible silence of midnight, the dressmaker awoke; a sound could be clearly heard in all the soundlessness, oh, she heard it only too clearly, and hearing it she believed she would lose her mind from terror. In the darkness someone was leafing through one of her fashion magazines. The woman, who had sat up in bed, wanted to scream out loud in fear, but fear itself suppressed her cry of fear, fright itself refused to emit a cry of fright. Terror itself, like a degenerate father choking his son, choked the scream of terror. Imagine that, dear reader, and now imagine how it climbed into bed with the dressmaker. It was Death who, in the stillness of midnight, paid a visit to the young woman so that he could embrace her with his cold arms, so that he could kiss her with his dreadful kiss. The next morning when someone came to see the dressmaker, he found her dead. She lay there dead in her bed.

1914

THE LANDSCAPE (I)

EVERYTHING was so eerie. No sky anywhere, and the earth was drenched. I was walking, and as I was walking I put the question before myself if it wouldn't be better to turn around and head back home. But an indefinite something beckoned me on, and I followed my path farther through the gloomy mist. I took pleasure in the infinite sorrow that prevailed all around. In the fog, in the grayness, my heart and imagination opened wide. Everything was so gray. I stood still, enthralled by the beauty in the unloveliness, bewitched by hope in the midst of this hopelessness. It seemed as if henceforth it would be impossible for me to hope for anything. Then again it appeared as if a sweet, unspeakable, enchanting happiness meandered through the sorrowful landscape, and I thought I heard sounds, but everything was still. There was another person stepping through the woods, through all this melancholy dark. His shrouded figure was even darker than the darkness of the landscape. Who was he, and what did he want? And soon other dark figures emerged, but none of the figures heeded the others, each seemed to have enough to do with himself alone. I, too, no longer cared what these people wanted or where they might be bound for in the darkness, cared only about myself, and set off into my own unclarity, which quickly embraced and clutched me close with its wet, cold arms. Oh, it seemed to me as if once I had been a king and now had to go as a beggar into the wide world that teemed with ignorance, that teemed there with an ominous thoughtlessness and indifference; it seemed as if it were eternally useless to be kind, eternally impossible to have honest intentions, as if everything were ludicrous and we were all only little children delivered beforehand into foolishness and impossibility.

Then, right after this, everything, everything was again good, and again I walked with an unutterably joyful spirit into the beautiful, devout darkness.

1914

WALKING

SOMEONE went walking. He could have taken a train and traveled into the distance, but he only wanted to ramble about nearby. Things near seemed to him more significant than significant and important distant things. Thus to him insignificance was significance. We don't wish to deny him this. He was called Tobold, but regardless whether he was called that or something else, he had little money in his pockets and a cheerful spirit in his heart. So he walked nicely, slowly forward, no friend to excessive speed. Haste he scorned; by rushing stormily along he would have only worked up a sweat. Why do that, he thought, and he marched slowly, carefully, agreeably, and moderately on. The steps he took were measured and tempered, the pace one of remarkable ease, the sun pleasantly scorching hot, which Tobold sincerely and genuinely welcomed. Yet he would also have gladly accepted a rain shower. Then he would have opened an umbrella and properly marched under the rain. He even longed for a bit of wetness, but since the sun shone, he took no exception to it. He was, in fact, one who almost never found fault with anything. Now he took his hat off his head to carry it in his hand. The hat was old. A certain journeyman-like faded-ness clearly characterized the hat. It was shabby yet nonetheless treated by the wearer with respect for the simple reason that memories were attached to it. Tobold always found it hard to part with well-worn and threadbare things. Thus, for example, at present he wore shoes that were torn. Certainly he could have bought a new pair of boots. That abundantly poor he was not. We don't want to depict him as totally destitute. But the shoes were old, full of memories, within them he had already walked many roads, and how faithfully they had endured so far. Tobold loved everything old, everything used and exhausted;

yes, sometimes he even adored antiquated things. For example, he loved old people, fairly worn-out old folk. Can anyone truly blame him? Hardly, since this is such a pretty streak of piety, isn't it? And so he step-by-stepped on out into the splendid, lovely blue. Oh, how blue the sky was, and how snowy white were the clouds. To behold clouds and sky again and again was a delight for Tobold. That's why he so much enjoyed traveling on foot, because the walker can take in everything so calmly, sumptuously, and freely, while nowhere can a train traveler stand still and pause, except in the station, where mostly elegant tail-coated waiters inquire whether one would like a glass of beer. Tobold would gladly forgo a few beers just to be free and left to walk with his legs, since his own legs delighted him and walking for him was a peaceful pleasure. Now a child bade him good morning and Tobold said good morning in return, and as he walked on, he thought long about the dear little child who had looked at him so prettily and smiled at him so enchantingly and who wished him such a friendly good morning.

1914

THE SHEPHERD

A CERTAIN someone is lying in the sun, though not quite. Under a tall tree his legs and lazybones feet are in the sun, and his head, a dreamful head, in the shade. He is a shepherd lying there half in sun and half in shadow; his animals graze not far away; he can leave them to themselves without worry. So he just lies there and doesn't really know what he should be thinking about. He is free to think about anything, and then again he has nothing he needs to be thinking about. Now he thinks about this, now that, now on this or that, now on something else. The thoughts come and go, appear before his mind and vanish again; they gather only to disperse, uniting into a great whole and disintegrating into tiny bits. The person lying there has time to think, time to be thoughtless and idle. Work might be nice and useful, but how much, how much nicer it is to do nothing, to dream and laze about all day, like the one sleeping there under a tall tree. Is he asleep? Oh, we imagine now and then his eyes close, overcome with drowsiness and fatigue from the pure pleasure of being, his senses fade, and he slumbers into sweet unconsciousness. Sleeping is lovely, but even more lovely is the soft, sweet reawakening; so now he falls asleep and now awakes again, and so to him the enchantress Time flows and fades and dissipates like the winds sweeping over the green plain, four o'clock, five o'clock, six and seven o'clock, until gradually evening comes on and a golden, pleasant darkness descends from the sky to the earth. Shepherd, sleeper who dreams away the time, are you happy? Yes, absolutely you are, you're happy. Dark thoughts you do not know nor want to know. If something evil ever comes to you, you just turn over on your side, or you pick up the instrument you always have with you and play music, and soon you're surrounded by a sunlit serenity again. Well, let's let him keep lying there. No one need worry about him. After all, he's no worry to himself either.

1914

THE INVITATION

I HAVE a marvelously beautiful little spot to show you, divine one. It lies completely hidden in the quiet, unassuming green forest, like a thought within a thought. It is a soft, mild ravine visited by no one. It lies so snuggly buried in the trees, ah, so sweetly concealed; there I fancy I want to kiss you with heartfelt, gentle, sweet, and long kisses, which interdict any discourse, even the most beautiful and best. The spot, as tender and remote as it is, no travel guide lists as a sight worth seeing. A small winding path through thick undergrowth leads to the ravine, to the place of magic where, miraculous one, I want to show you how much I love you, where, dear angel, I want to show you how I adore you. There caressing and embracing occur as if by themselves, and lips touch as if by themselves. You have no idea yet how I can kiss. Come, then, to this place where there is nothing but the lovely rustling of the tall trees, there you'll experience it. I won't speak a word, nor will you, we'll both be silent, only the leaves will whisper softly and through the delicate branches the sweet sunshine will break. Oh, how silent, how still it will be when we kiss, how beautiful it will be when our lips, thirsty and hungry for love, cling to one another, how sweet it will be when we make love in this silent, dear ravine. We want to caress and kiss one another without end, until evening comes and with it the silver, twinkling stars and the moon, the heavenly moon. We will have nothing to say, since everything should be only an unbroken, hours-long, enchanting kiss. Whoever wants to love no longer wants to speak, because whoever wants to speak no longer wants to love. Oh, come to this holy, entranced place of deed, of act, where everything dissolves in fulfillment and everything drowns and dies in love. The birds with their gay song will tweet all around and the night surround us in heavenly silence. What we call the world will lie behind us and be held captive by its enchantment, we will both be children of the earth and feel what love means and feel what life means. Those who don't love have no existence, are not there, are dead. Those who have the desire to love rise from the dead, only the ones who love are alive.

1914

SUNDAY MORNING

TODAY, Sunday, I went out early into the nearby countryside. In our region, town and country touch one another like two good, valiant friends. I took only a hundred steps, or perhaps a hundred more, and there, laid out before me, was the rustic, delicate winter with its tousled trees and its lovely meadow-green. I came to the forest standing there so beautiful, so quiescent in the cold gray air with the graceful tips of its fir trees. From a distant village the Sunday bells loudly and yet gently and quietly rang over the land to the edge of the forest. Cold and the path frozen hard and a large, handsome farmhouse in the maze of blackish winter trees. A delicate, peaceful smoke rose from the chimney as if smiling, and a small, merry, jaunty path meandered through the field into the forest. I walked past people dressed in their Sunday best into my old beloved forest of wonder, and later out the other side again, where again I was met by path and field, gray sky, tree and house and other people. In the winter cold and winter deadness there was so much warm peace, so much ancient and eternally rejuvenated and joyful life. A green rise looked roguishly down at me. I love, love my country with its paths, corners, districts, and nooks. Soon I was at home again in my pleasantly heated room. I sat down at the table, took up my pen, and wrote this.

1914

THE MOON

YESTERDAY was a wonderfully beautiful moonlit night, so quiet, mild, and still, as though the whole world had sunk into a dark, sweet enchantment. I walked through the narrow lanes and little alleyways. Many people were out and about, as if the magic of the moon had drawn them from their homes into the open. The streets were all smooth and soft and bright in the moonlight, and everything so hushed and friendly. A measured joy radiated through every street; moreover, on this beautiful night the Christmas market was going on and the city was alive with people. I walked through a little narrow garden lane that nestled alongside a mountain. There the magic was overwhelming. It was like a fairy tale. —The rocky ground reverberated under every footstep. Slowly I walked on. After each step I took, I stood still and turned around to look up at the heavenly, beautiful, gentle moon and the fir trees and the ancient city towers. The stars, like amorous glances, trembled and shimmered between the sleevelike fir twigs bending upward. Soon I was on top of the mountain which rose over the cozy town like an old giant. Steps hewn into the white rock led me up and, having reached the top, I looked down into a soft, mysterious, gentle depth that was like a vision in a dream. I went up even farther through the forest, which was completely white. Everything was white from the moon, so pale and lovely. I thought of Father and Mother; a nameless, tender, femininely anxious, fainthearted feeling crept over me. I wished I could stand in the moonlit night forever and surrender to old, dear thoughts, to stay like this forever and be able to think back on the past. The dark-bright sky with its white cottony clouds appeared to me like a beautiful, beloved, lush meadow. The moon resembled a dreamy shepherd, the soft clouds little lambs, and the stars blinking forth now and then from underneath were like flowers. Music and the sound of voices penetrated up from the town below. I felt unspeakably solemn. It seemed to me as though the entire expanding quiet night was a bodily creature and the moon its soul. For quite some time I remained standing there.

1914

STROLL (I)

I TOOK a pleasant little appetizing stroll, quite easily and enjoyably it unfolded. I walked through a village, then through a kind of ravine, then through a forest, then over a field, then again through a village, then over an iron bridge, under which the wide, sunny green river flowed past, then kept walking slowly beside the river and kept on until it was evening. But first I have to return to the forest. It's quite likely, by the way, that I'll have more to say about the bridge, too. In the forest it was so devoutly still, so solemn, and as I came out of the damp, dark, green fir forest, I saw two children at the edge who had gathered wood, and they had such bright faces and arms. The winter sun cast a mild, golden, magical radiance over the fields on the hills, over verdant meadows and dark-brown farmland. Bare black trees stood in the sun. Then I saw, as I was just walking along, a new child's face, a sweet one that smiled at me. And then, as I said, I came again to the bridge which glimmered and flickered all over in the gold and silver of the sun. Lovely and stupendously the water flowed under the bridge. Later, on the country road, I met a woman whom I remember because she greeted me so kindly. Then I thought: "What a pleasure it is to be permitted to be among people." The houses on the other side of the river stood so beautifully, so openly on the green rise, and the windows were filled with a yellow luster. A flock of birds flew into the blazing evening glow. I followed the skein with my eyes until it vanished. One side of the world was calm and warm and dark, the other cold and golden and glisteningly bright. Calmly, step by step, I walked on, until I took a turn into the countryside. There I saw some people, a woman and a child under twilight-darkish trees. Their eyes stared at me so quizzically. Then I walked past a house that stood alone in an open, expansive field, a delicate, marvelously strange, old, lovely little garden before or beside it. The little garden was fenced in by a whimsical, fantastical hedge. Now, all at once, everything became dream, love, and fantasy. Everything I beheld now took on an august and elevated form. The region itself seemed to poeticize, to fantasize. It seemed to be dreaming about its own beauty. The land was sunk in deep reflection. I stood still, bewitched by the beauty surrounding me, and looked attentively all around. Evening had fallen, the green spoke a lovely vesperal language. Colors are like languages. The roof of the house, beside which I stood, drooped over the windows like a hat over eyes. Aren't windows a house's eyes? Now I had to look up at the half-moon standing high over the forest mountain. It seemed wondrous how the dark earth lay there so warm, so companionable, so blissfully calm, and how the moon above hung poised and shone in the opalescently pale, cold, celestial solitude. Its color was a sharp, ice-cold silver-green. Divinely beautiful and inexpressibly dark stood the forest with its lovely fir tips under the graceful sovereign, the glorious moon. I went past another house, a woman stood in the doorway and a kitten huddled beside her. In my mind I entered the house and stayed to live with them. "How akin to one another are people and houses," I said to myself. It turned darker and darker. Evenings are divinities, and in the evening it's as if one were in a sweet, lofty, abundantly melancholy church. In the pale sky there now stood a delightful blazing red. It was as though the sky were a cheek blushing from happiness and bliss. A country lad was leading a brown cow past me. From out of the expanding dusk the little village children gave forth a truly wonderful "Good evening." Every face was glowing reddish from the rosy glow of sunset. Already the stars were coming out. There happened to be an inn along the road. I went in.

1914

LITTLE SNOW LANDSCAPE

YESTERDAY we had some snow, and today in the early morning hours I went out for a close and calm inspection of the snow-covered landscape. Winsome, like a good little kitten that's just groomed itself, the rich, lovely countryside now rests there. Every child, I should think, can understand at heart the beauty of a snowy landscape, the fine clean whiteness is so easy to comprehend, so childlike. Something angelic is lying over the earth, and a sweet, attractive innocence is whitely and greenly spread out there. I delighted in my task, my pleasurable duty, that obliged me to take careful notice of the snow and its enticements. A wonderful subtlety and beauty lay in the fact that the grass so agreeably and with such delicate tips looked out from the field of snow. I walked again to my old immutable, benevolent enchanter, the forest, into it and out again as in a dream, and there it was, the land of my childhood in the colors of my childhood. The little trees and big trees seemed to perform a graceful dance on the white field, and the houses wore white caps, hats, headpieces, or roofs. It looked so scrumptious, so alluring, so gay and so dear, just like the delicate, sweet art of a skillful confectioner. Morning light shone in a window, and an exquisite house stood at some distance with windows like eyes that blinked joyfully and slyly. The house was like a face and the five green windows were its eyes. Why not go there, dear reader, while the enchanting country view is still standing there with snow on its lovely face? One should never be too lackadaisical and fear a few hundred steps, get out of your lazybones bed early, stand up on your pins and walk out just a little way so the eye can gaze its fill and the heart, craving freedom, can breathe. Go to the gracious snowy landscape that smiles at you as if with a nice, friendly mouth. Smile back and give it my best regards.

1914

SUMMER NIGHT

IT WAS midnight. A young man sat in his room by his lamp reading *Faust*, but while he was reading, now and then he weighed whether he should continue or go out into the street. It was so beautiful outside, the moon shone so brightly. A sheet of paper with writing on it lay next to the young man's book. The page appeared to be the beginning of a letter, perhaps one of those letters during whose assiduous recording one comes to a standstill in the middle of writing, arrested by various strange doubts. The young man stood up from the table and stepped to the open window through which the night wind, like an easeful, friendly thought, blew into the wide, bright room. Earlier, while reading, he had heard the steps of countless strollers from below. As he was reading, he had, in fact, already been amidst the people down there, walking quietly up and down. Now he looked out the window that lay, as it were, in the air high over the street, down at the peaceful nocturnal picture below that moved back and forth over the quiet square, and he smiled at his moonlit garret solitude, at his contented aloneness which seemed to him as beautiful as or perhaps more beautiful than anything else. Surely he would have gladly been walking along close behind one of the fashionable, attractive beauties, for example behind Frau L., so as to admire her figure and lovely movements. Gladly he would have joined in the general evening walk, his steps easily mingling with the steps of the others, yet he felt just as happy or perhaps much happier the way things were, and thus he stayed seated at the window. "Wonderful night," he said quietly to himself, "how beautiful you are, and you, heavenly moon, how beautiful you are." From a beer garden located right beneath the youth's window, a flute and violin concert, with sweet attacks, happy weeping, melancholy exuberance, giggles, laughter, and a nightingale-like lament, resounded as an enchanting musical flirting, as the play of waves and reflections of life up to his attentive ears. The young man adored the sounds, he was intoxicated by them. Gradually it grew quieter down on the street. The lodger doused the lamp. He wanted only the lovely moonlight for company.

1915

CHRISTMAS

OUR CITY is lovely, especially because it lies right against a wooded mountain. Today, toward evening, I walked briskly up into the forest where I encountered three real Father Christmas woodsmen carrying fir trees over their shoulders. I wouldn't have missed meeting them for the world. Already from afar I heard their voices echoing through the evening and the wintry forest. How primeval they looked with their beards and swarthy faces.

Then I came down into the city set so tightly against the mountain one almost wants to call it a forest and mountain town. To thus emerge from the quiet, dark, wide forest onto the steep, rocky path and then down the steps and immediately into the city that's so warm, close, and sudden, how nice, how truly heartening this was. Nowhere can I imagine nature and city so charmingly coupled and conjoined as it is for us here. And then how snugly the houses encircle us in the city. One walks as though in a fortress where everything is confined and near to everything else, the town hall with the town square, upper lane and lower alley, and the towering old good church, and all around the smaller side alleys with their dark corners and niches. And then the pleasant, friendly figures, the calm faces. Brighter and darker figures, bright and dark patches. Then you walk across an ancient square, a former moat dreamily still and lovely and quiet, here and there a roof, a dashing gable, a lantern, a fortress tower as ancient as the hills.

And the winter night so gentle, with such dark, good, peaceful, honest eyes. And the old, eternally beautiful thought as well that soon it will and should be Christmas within these walls, where in every spirit and in every human heart an oddly sweet, heavy, and light burden shall fall, where every eye sees its Christmas tree and Christmas candle, and all the narrow and wide streets ring and are redolent with peace, with pleasant forgiveness, and with every beautiful, sincere reconciliation. Oh, how lovely, how large-eyed, gentle, and mellow our city is at this quiet time of winter, this quiet time of evening, in this sweet, quiet, beloved Christmas time. Every shop window abounds with the prettiest things. From the street one sees the butcher standing in the butcher shop, the baker in the bakery, the milkman in the creamery. Every shop is aglow, especially the toy stores that speak to the hearts of children. This evening, as I said, I came down from the forest into the city and became completely enamored, completely enchanted by it.

1915

HÖLDERLIN

HÖLDERLIN had begun to write poems, but galling poverty forced him to go to Frankfurt am Main to earn his living as a private tutor in a family. In this respect, this magnificent, beautiful soul is in the same bind as a laborer's. He had to sell his fervent propensity for freedom, suppress his regal, colossal pride. The result of this harsh necessity was a convulsion, a perilous shaking within.

He repaired to an attractive, elegant prison.

Born to wander in dreams and imagination and hang on the neck of nature, to while away the days and nights blissfully writing poetry under the thick canopy of innocent trees, to converse with the meadow and its flowers, to gaze up at the sky and observe the divinely serene procession of the clouds—and now he stepped into the pristine, bourgeois confines of a wealthy private home and assumed the duty so appalling to his rebellious energy of having to behave honestly, cleverly, and politely.

He felt intense dread. He thought himself lost, squandered, and he was. Yes, he was lost because he didn't have the pitiful strength to renounce shamefully all of his delicious fluids and forces that ought to be disavowed and disguised.

There, there he snapped, was torn to shreds, and from then on was a poor, pathetic invalid.

Hölderlin, capable of thriving only in freedom, saw his bliss annihilated because his freedom was lost. He tugged and strained against the chains he was clasped in, only wounding himself; the shackles were unbreakable.

A hero lay in chains, a lion had to be well behaved and mannerly, a

Greek royal moved about in a bourgeois room whose tight, tiny, prettily tapestried walls crushed his prodigious brain.

It was here that the miserable mental disintegration already began, that slow, soft, terrible smashing of all clarity. From hopelessness to hopelessness, from one soul-shredding trembling and dread to another, his desolate thoughts roamed and lurched. It was like a soundless, still, torpid shattering of celestially bright worlds.

The world to him grew murky, coarse, and dark, and in order to at least get drunk on dalliance and delusion, to forget the boundless grief of lost freedom, to overcome the sorrow of the enslaved tethered lion pacing up and down in his cage, desperately up and down, up and down, it dawned on him to fall in love with Madame. This diverted him, suited him, did his annihilated, strangled, suffocated heart good, if only for moments at a time.

While the one and only thing he loved was the sunken dream of freedom, he imagined he loved the lady. As if in a wasteland, desolation surrounded his consciousness.

When he smiled, he felt as though in order to bring the smile to his lips he had to drag it out painstakingly from a deep, craggy cave.

Morbidly, he longed to return to his childhood, to return to be born anew and become a boy again; he wished he were dying. He wrote, "When I was a boy..." One knows the glorious song.

While the person within him despaired and his essence bled from numerous miserable wounds, his artistry ascended to great heights like a dancer opulently dressed, and whenever Hölderlin felt he was perishing, he made music and rapturously wrote poems. He sang of the destruction and dismantling of his life on the instrument of language which he spoke in golden, wonderful tones. He lamented over his rights and his broken happiness like only kings are capable of lamenting, with a pride, a sovereignty the likes of which were unknown in the domain of poetry.

Powerful, fateful hands tore him from the world, its circumstances much too small for him, and over the edge of the knowable into madness, where with the force of a giant he descended into its light-drenched, rich in will-o'-the-wisps, meek, kind abyss to slumber forever in sweet dissipation and obscurity.

"It's utterly impossible, Hölderlin," said the mistress of the house, "and what you want is unthinkable. Everything you think always goes beyond all that is decent and possible, and everything you say tears asunder all that's obtainable. You can't and won't be well. Well-being means too little to you, and the peace of limitations is too common for you. Everything for you is and will always be an abyss, a limitlessness. You and the world are an ocean.

"What can and may I say to calm you when you reject as contemptible everything that might comfort you? Everything cramped and small bewilders you, makes you ill; everything vast and unbounded jerks you up and down; where nothing abides, there's no reveling. Patience is unworthy of you, but impatience cuts you to pieces. You're respected, loved, and pitied, and thus there's no joy for you.

"Since nothing pleases you, what should I do?

"You love me?

"I don't believe it, must forbid myself to believe it, and wish you would forbid yourself to make me believe it. You're not compelled to love me, otherwise you would be able to be calm, kind, and happy, and be patient with yourself and me. I have no right to think I mean much to you.

"Do be gentle, agreeable, and intelligent. Soon I'll only fear you, and that's a feeling I deplore. Why don't you let go of your passion and rise above yourself? How beautiful, warm, and great you could be if you made a determined effort to do that. But your audacious fancies are killing you, and the dream you make of life robs you of life. Listen, couldn't the renunciation of greatness not also be greatness?

"Everything is so painful."

Thus she spoke to him. Then Hölderlin went forth from the house, continued to wander about in the world for a while, and thereafter sank into incurable madness.

1915

WÜRZBURG

A WHILE back, that is, around a few years ago, I believe I journeyed one beautiful summer's day on foot from Munich to Würzburg. A nimble, foolish, inexperienced young man, namely I myself, simply flew along there. The weather was hot and magnificent. The spectacle of the world was a kind of mixture of blue, yellow, and green. Blue was the high, bright, wide sky, green were the forests through which I walked or whooshed past, and yellow the lush fields of grain stretching out on both sides of the wide country road. Another lovely, very significant color was white, because flying along with the hurrying wanderer and industriously walking country lad, albeit not on the hard earth but high up in the air, were white summer clouds like huge, powerful ships sailing the blue ocean. Since I was in the habit year in and year out of being short of cash, the little bit of money I carried with me didn't bother me at all. On my feet I wore a kind of gymnast's shoe made of canvas and thus strode through the region as light as the wind and as untethered as free thought. It seemed as if the wind wanted to sweep and chase me away, so swiftly was I hurrying on.

In Munich I had gotten to know quite well a few literary personalities of some distinction and importance, but I had strange, oppressive feelings at these artistic and literary gatherings for which I wasn't really suited. I no longer recall the exact facts and circumstances, only this: from every salon where subtleties and *excusés* dominated, I was driven out into the open world where wind, weather, crude words, harsh, brusque manners, and every thoughtlessness and coarseness reign. Young and impatient as I was, I couldn't stand the air of refined serenity. All the irreproachable, unswerving, tip-top, elegant behavior mainly instilled in me only sorrow and a kind of fear. Beneficent, great, almighty God, how lovely it is to walk in summer on your hot, vast, still earth, and with the most beautifully conjoined honest thirst and hunger. Everything so calm and bright and the world so boundless.

The hiking suit I wore had, as it were, something of southern Italy about it. It was a sort or species of suit that would have been impressive in Naples. In well-thought-out, well-measured Germany, however, it seemed to arouse more suspicion than trust, more aversion than affection. How audacious and fantastic I was at twenty-three.

With a boldly and, if possible, ingeniously sketching pencil and some light, casual, snappy firing-up of some colors, I want to go over the trip quickly.

My memory has faithfully retained: a group of imposing farm buildings standing in the bright sunlight; a troop or merry community of traveling and roaming young journeymen; a green, heavily armed, but in fact polite and benevolent country policeman who eyed and examined my passport and papers; multitudes of milestones or kilometerstones; a convivial inn or invitingly hospitable guesthouse where in the open air, under thick, tranquil garden green, I consumed a light-brown, delightful, enchanting schnitzel; wide stretches of verdant, flat country; a tattered, rickety, dilapidated, twisted, desolate, lonely homestead or house with a highly picturesque, poetic, tattered disorderliness in front of it; an overabundance of midday heat, a small acacia grove near a rural town, the loneliness and remoteness of it; a proud castle, country manor, estate, or imperious knight's castle in the dazzlingly bright, scintillatingly hot landscape; a totally odd, fantastic, curious, peculiar old town with a seventeenth-century flair, through whose narrow, hushed, languorous, fabulous alleys that swam in the movingly beautiful golden light of the summer evening I strode quietly as if through a dream, as if through the melancholy example of the remaining, once vigorous inflorescence itself, as if through evidence of the incredible; dropping in on various cavernous, gloomy pubs where dark, thick beers were served, stepping out of dives and drinking halls back onto the street; a lazy, blackish river, and later again a town, along with various other things.

Würzburg is a city exceptionally well worth seeing. Upon finally arriving there, after valiantly enduring and suffering all sorts of hardships, the first thing I did was to enter a barbershop to get a proper shave, because I vividly felt and sensed that there really could be more than one reason for me to acquire some elegance. Secondly, in an upscale shoe store I bought a pair of fine new boots since the shoes I had on seemed, at their best, fit for causing the highest mistrust, contempt, and suspicion. Thirdly, I felt myself drawn, driven, and heartily moved to go and eat lunch, and accordingly, with astonishing impudence, with the cool and calm bearing of a consular attaché, and with the determined mien of a resolutely victorious or death-defying conqueror of grievances, difficulties, and obstacles, stepped into the world's finest and foremost hotel restaurant.

When they saw me, the people seemed in shock.

"You there, sir, before you dare enter, would you have the courtesy to state what it is you want here?"

With this rather brusque and challenging request, a dark-suited, genteelly clad gentleman, apparently the manager himself, darted forth at the aggressor and invader, but no matter how courageous or even heroically brave the defense that was put up to protect this in fact strongly and vehemently threatened citadel or position, it was of no use anymore. Its adversary was too powerful.

Who was none other than—to wit—me! I responded:

"What do I want here, you ask? How is it possible to ask that at such great length when anyone with a sliver of worldly experience must see at a glance that it's a case of hunger, indeed, of frank, honest hunger and the elimination of the same, and with the greatest possible haste? What do I want? I want to eat! Here, as I see it, is a venue where the most sophisticated bourgeois and aristocratic ladies and gentlemen are accustomed to dine, fetch and find refreshment. Since I, too, now, to the utmost degree, as it seems to me, am in need of a rest and repletion of my hunger, I enter your premises, with your permission, for I believe it shouldn't take me a hundred years to ponder whether or not this might be a suitable establishment for me. Don't inconvenience yourself on my account. Kindly make room. With such a noble, superb, and substantial appetite as mine at the moment absolutely is, it's my opinion and expressed view, based on simple, poor common sense, that I should be allowed and required to enter each and every, even the finest and most distinguished house."

Already I had stormed in and, amidst feasting high nobility and other notable banqueting elite, had taken my seat. The restaurant teemed with formidable beaks and contemptuous looks from eyes behind gripped spectacles. The hall possessed a chilly beauty. I, as I let myself be served like an imperial count, was the certainly not at all edifying object of everyone's attention. My exquisite young vagabond nature shone splendidly in the midst of the choicest selection imaginable of the cream of society. I remember it with delight even today, because youth is inimitable and only when young do we have the serene comfort to cheerfully carry out such gleeful pranks. Our mischievous youthful jests are really not the best, but certainly not the worst things in our lives.

Since such a lavish and boastful way of life, given his sparse and miserable means, obviously had to tear a horrible hole in his meager, paltry funds and undermine and pitifully bore through the entirety of the wealth at his disposal, the bold man of the world and bon vivant now felt compelled to spend the night wistfully and miserably in one of the most wretched inns his eyes had ever beheld. About the unpleasantnesses in the form of small, charming, nice, engaging members of the animal night-kingdom that came in many guises and pounced upon him during the night, as he lay in the awful, rock-hard hostel bed, to bestow their attentions and socialize with him, albeit in an most peculiar way, he'd rather not waste too many words, as he is of the extremely commendable opinion that elaborate description and reference would, in this case, be rather indelicate.

Abruptly I got up and stepped to the open window. It was midnight, and instead of the sleep that I wasn't allowed to savor because malevolent, tiny, cute villains robbed me of it, I savored and enjoyed the view of the most beautiful moonlit night, like an Eichendorff moon casting down from on high all of its inexpressible beauty, its magical, mild, pale grace, its divine softness here and there and everywhere, like rain drizzling on dark rooftops, on towers and peaked gables soaring high above. A gentle concertina played, and wonderful, in fact heavenly, was the nocturnal stillness spread all around, this bright, childlike, moonlit-night stillness, this deep, sweet, midnight magic, this dark-bright, peaceful moonglow, this music of solemnity, kindness, and happiness, this sonata to joy, this moonlight sonata! Doesn't Beethoven's work of art live in every beautiful moonlit night? Don't all the best works of art always originate in simplicity and the ordinary? Indeed, isn't a moonlit night also only something quotidian that's bestowed upon beggar and prince alike?

When it began to turn day, I readily—understandably so—left my hostel and, going down onto the street, took off in search of Dauthendey, whose acquaintance I had made in Munich and who at the time was living in Würzburg.

After I had spent the entire morning arduously asking around and searching for the address of the gentleman, believing myself entitled, imprudently as well as whimsically, evincing the utmost obstinacy, to inquire at random of unknown people who either were looking unsuspectingly out of just any old low-lying window or happening casually by on the street, as to the writer's address, a technique that, albeit seemingly adventurous, eventually turned me surly, until at last I found him. He was still lounging peacefully in bed. When he saw me, he laughed.

"Just look at you," he exclaimed in a loud voice, and as he got out of bed and dressed with a diligence worth observing, he addressed the following wise speech to me, which I shall forthwith impart:

"Your attire, my dear friend, is much too quixotic. Wait, I'll take a look. You'll have to put on something else immediately right here in my house, since articles of clothing like those worn by you are walked around in in Arcadia or some other imaginary country but in no way in reality or in our day and age. You have to learn how better to understand the times in which you are allowed to live. You can be as adventurous as you like on the inside, but you let your inwardness, your disposition, your soul be all too obviously noticeable. You like to exhibit in public your fantasizing and dreaming. That's not smart. Look, here's a suit you could wear anytime without causing umbrage. Why be so conspicuous, when you most certainly in no way want to be? Without a doubt you're simply strikingly inept, and since that's the case, or seems to be, permit me, if you will, to give you a proper little lesson on these matters.

"You look like an inhabitant of a region that exists, at most, nowhere but in your head, whereas you would be well advised to appear like a simple, poor human being among other human beings, a contemporary among your contemporaries. Surely you won't hold these words against me but realize that I'm right and then kindly submit to what I'm saying, as you are an intelligent person and it's obvious it's only your fierce youthful obstinacy that makes you such a peculiar figure. But there's no point whatsoever in your appearing peculiar and weird. Such a manner of distinguishing yourself must be considered entirely bogus. Regarding distinction, our tenet must be that it's strictly imperative we become conspicuous only through our abilities. We can come up with any number of rules and regulations about this, but we're not allowed to take liberties, or only a few. So! Now onward—and cheerfully strip off that superfluous pretense of outlandishness. If you have odd feelings and thoughts, that's more than enough. No one need see that you're strange and unique, that you have imagination and a taste for the bizarre. Otherwise, you'll only be misjudged everywhere with your unconventionality and every step of the way be an annoyance to yourself, which you can't possibly welcome."

While he spoke, or had spoken, he pulled items from his overflowing and overstocked wealth of clothes in his wardrobe and chest of drawers and, one by one, handed me a coat, pants, a shirt, a vest, a hat, and a white starched detachable collar, in addition to some of the nicest bow ties, neckties, and cravats, handing them to me in succession, thus forcing me to put on all of them and in doing so transform myself into a totally different and new person. When the transition and swift transformation had been completed, my master, friend, and kind patron exclaimed, "Now you look splendid! Come along. Let us take a little walk."

And in fact, we set off together in good and cheerful spirits for a stroll in the streets, where in the nicest summer weather that smiled gaily at us numerous members of the public promenaded back and forth. In my new outfit I felt like a prince, by which I am attempting to convey that I almost felt reborn. To be sure, the elegant high collar restricted and pinched me a little; nevertheless, I gladly made the not-too-egregious sacrifice to the tenets of propriety and the demands of the leaders of fashion and renounced with pleasure a small portion of personal well-being or comfort. It was the first starched collar I had ever worn in my life. Since my behavior almost instantly, as it were, obligingly adapted itself to the handsome things I had the honor to wear, I was carefully measured and eyeballed from all sides by, so to speak, friendly and respectful eyes, which by no means necessarily put me in a bad frame of mind. Surely from far or near my straw, or leisure, or distinguished summer or rustic hat indeed resembled a journeyman's. Dauthendey, however, told me I should simply stay calm; according to every reasonable person's considered opinion the headgear I wore couldn't be more admirable and advantageous. Concern was unbecoming and any doubt was, to a high degree, unsuitable, as was to doubt the hat in question that harmonized well with, befitted, and suited me.

Soon we went down into one of Würzburg's numerous wine cellars and pubs, where we let ourselves be served all sorts of food and drink in the most pleasurable manner. It was splendid to sit and chat in a cool, shadowy, fragrant, quiet corner.

Eight days, no longer, but also no less, I stayed under the kind protection of my friend in the beautiful city of Würzburg, on which I think back with tremendous joy. Würzburg's inhabitants seemed serene and at the same time industrious, gregarious, and polite. While some of the streets were magnificent, offering an exalted view, I found the traffic brisk. You could see the whole town's layout entangled and enveloped in copious green parkways. Far and wide extended the pleasant, benevolently rustling, suffused-with-liberality paths on which it was well worth one's while to stroll. Sometimes Dauthendey brought me to a country house that was gracefully situated on top of a vineyard, where I was allowed to meet all sorts of affable and sophisticated people who granted the noble right of hospitality a palpably open, agreeable playground.

Among other places, we visited together the castle or palace of the prince-bishops, where we admired Tiepolo's glorious fresco, in addition to various other treasures and beautiful works. Slowly and attentively we walked through each and every awe-inspiring hall where once a dynasty of princes lived given to lavishness and extravagance. Luxurious splendor merged with the most charming taste, and the most delicate style with voluptuous, capricious wealth. The castle itself appeared to our astonished eyes fantastically huge; its phenomenal dimensions visibly reminded us of the quite quintessentially terrible omnipotence of the former princes. The extensive ornate court garden seemed to us like a fairy tale. Even from the outside, kings and princes were adept at appearing regal, and whoever then set foot in the bewildering splendor of the interior was bowed and paralyzed by the superiority of the fabulously beautiful view and had to recognize at once that, compared to princely dignity, he was only a poor, weak, insignificant subject abiding in humility and obedience, fated to quietly suffer every severe, unreasonable imposition, every humiliating, degrading condition, if not perhaps finally even to love it.

Eight enchanting summer days it was. Dauthendey asked if I still had money. "No," I answered. That's what he thought, he replied with a most understanding smile, and then gave me a tiny bit. He didn't have much himself. The finances of artists are usually pretty catastrophic, a regrettable situation that nevertheless can't impede the ones in question from affectionately and unabashedly sharing like brothers. Also, they don't reflect long before taking what's offered.

Didn't I, for instance, go bathing in the River Main? Most definitely! And at this opportunity the old, imposing, statue-adorned Main Bridge, one of Würzburg's sights, must be mentioned. Didn't one sit pleasurably at night in the concert garden under the thickly leaved branches of tall trees with a glass of wine or beer to listen in absolute delight to Mozartian or other sounds? The series of beautiful mild nights that followed, one upon the other, was glorious, on one of which, because of having been delayed, I was denied entrance into the guesthouse. I spent the night on one of the park benches under the open sky. A watchman, nocturnally patrolling up and down, keenly and long observed the overnighter liberally lodging in the Hotel of Lovely Nature, probably because he felt obliged to figure out whether the nocturnalizer dreaming in front of him was a scoundrel and, as such, a danger to the public, or an honest person and, as such, a benefit to society. The next day I was drowsy. Strange faces, visions, forms, among them figures, like Romeo in Shakespeare's *Romeo and Juliet* without a head, glowed dark red against the sunny blue day under the luminous sky before me. My somnolent, or better, my not-having-slept-enough eyes gazed into a glowing Orient, into a fantasyland, and the ground on which I walked, or at least seemed to be sufficiently bound and determined to walk in an orderly fashion, was spinning dreamily around me.

Anyway, I must have well-nigh struck myself as an errant tramp and lollygagger, and because such a bad impression thoroughly displeased me, I found it secretly not in the least inadvisable, little by little, to resolve to set a solemn goal sometime soon to counter such an idle way of life and accordingly redirect Mr. Count or Mr. Lazybones, if he would be so gracious as to agree with the necessary correction and kindly scrap any possible convenient objections to getting back onto more diligent paths.

Did I not in a chestnut grove above a sunny riverbank as pretty as a picture dine on and devour the best country hotcakes with a scrumptious green salad? Most certainly! And didn't I see myself making small talk with a Russian woman studying fine arts and painting in Munich, with a dark-skinned as well as dark-eyed American woman, and with a real, true, genuine, lorgnette-armed privy councilor? Didn't I, idler and squanderer of summertime, write a rather long, intimate, passionate poem into a lady's poetry album? No doubt! And, indeed, why on earth not? And didn't I, on the whole, play a totally useless, pointless, untenable, irresponsible, and thus superfluous part? Absolutely!

I was overcome by a seriousness of purpose and decided to depart, to journey farther into the world. With every stroll I felt an unnameable longing for a sensible human destiny, however harsh it might prove to be. To an extraordinary degree it drove me toward order and daily work, and I well-nigh yearned for nothing more vigorously than finding and fulfilling some duty.

"I have to ask you for twenty marks," I said to Dauthendey, as we walked together through the quiet midnight alleys for the last time, each of us alone with his thoughts, "so I can leave early tomorrow morning for Berlin."

Right away he gave me the money. A dubious lantern illuminated the peculiar business and the pensive, lonely scene.

"I thank you; because, you see: a destiny commands me and I must leave. Laugh at me if you want, that won't stop me at all from feeling what I'm saying to you is serious. I assume that somewhere there is an honest struggle for life awaiting me, which I thus must seek. In the long run I can't bear indolent beauty, mild, gentle summer pleasures, tarrying, lingering, or dithering, since I don't seem cut out for that. Instead, I'm filled with wondrous, dangerous ideas and imbued with the fortunate conviction that tells me I'm capable of forging ahead through the world and its ruthlessness, of muddling through to the point where I will encounter proper work and a higher purpose. I see you're smiling—doubtless you do that because you find my language extraordinarily lofty. But I find that life should contain a certain tone, a vehemence, and I believe there are people who can't live without the taste of adventure. Farewell!

"I imagine Berlin is the city that will either see me wrecked and destroyed or develop and flourish. I need a city where the rough, fierce struggle for life reigns. Such a city will be good for me, will invigorate me. Such a city will favor and at the same time tame me. Such a city will make me conscious of the fact that I'm probably not entirely without good traits. In Berlin, after a short or long while, I'll learn to my true delight what the world wants from me and what, for my part, I am expected to ask of it. Already I half feel and see it, but it's still vague. In Berlin it'll be clear to me; one evening or early one morning in Berlin, I'll know it with hoped-for clarity. It's necessary to act, to take risks! In Berlin, in the midst of the maelstrom and turmoil and all the unrest and excitement of cosmopolitan life, in the intense bustle and activity, I'll find my peace. I'm positive about what I'm saying and that I'll experience what I'm talking about."

Dauthendey did indeed, as a friend, try to persuade me to cancel the trip, but the next morning, despite all his attempts to dissuade me, I sat in the train carrying me away into uncertainty.

Ah, it's glorious to reach a decision and, full of confidence, be heading toward the unknown.

1915

THE WORKER

HE WAS, in his way, a gentle, precious person. He was educated. Certain people acquire an unusual education in a most unique fashion.

His lowly station allowed him to go about in simple clothes. No one esteemed him, no one took any notice of him. He considered this fine, in fact delighted in it.

He walked calmly and quietly along, as it were, dark-bright, joyful, contemplative paths alongside delicate life. He extolled his modest situation.

A book meant weeks, often months of real pleasure for him. Spirits and thoughts accompanied him amicably, almost like kindhearted women. He lived more in the spirit than in the world; he lived a double life.

Nature, with its richly varied images, afforded him bright days and dark nights filled with an abundance of quiet pleasures.

The young worker became accustomed to feeling a deep gratitude, with which he happily went to bed in the evenings. With a similar feeling he rose early in the morning to go to his daily work.

Why, by the way, do we call him a "worker"? From whimsicality, fantasticalness, or contrariness? Are we of the opinion that we're characterizing him accurately? Why not?

For forty rappen he lunched in a kind of soup kitchen. If we've been properly informed, the food there was watery, choice, sparse, and meager.

He lived as quietly as a soldier, less for his sake than for something else, he wasn't clear what, but it sufficed to feel it snatch him up gently into a kind of sublimity.

In the evening he was always dreamy, and the night with its wonderful darkness he found divinely beautiful.

Nobody told him this. Nobody put ideas in his head. All enchanting, worthwhile thoughts descended from the air, from near and far, to surrender themselves and their sustenance to him.

His outward appearance did not in the least betray his tender inner needs. His manner presaged no air whatsoever of lofty humanity.

In time his knowledge became more and more refined. Only now and then, on the right occasion, did he speak openly and let it be felt who and what he was.

His secret was his continuous pleasure. His feelings were the silent source and fountain of an oddly covert delight.

Regarding his sociopolitical opinions, he was too solitary to be able to have something of the sort. Nor did he need any. He preferred to think of Father and Mother, of nature, of dear living things rather than politics. You might say he was romantic.

Thus, for example, poor worker that he was, he loved the palaces, the affectations, the proud, opulent appearance of the rich. He adored everything beautiful. He loved women, children, old and young people, lanes, houses.

Perhaps along with what is upright and good he also loved what is evil, and along with the beautiful what is not beautiful. Good and evil, beauty and ugliness seemed inseparable to him.

In this way he lived and loved. There was a certain nobility in him.

On one occasion he composed the following:

TWO LITTLE PROSE PIECES

I.

The people there are friendly. They have the beautiful need to ask one another if they can be of assistance. They don't walk past each other indifferently nor do they bother one another. They are affectionate but not inquisitive, approach but don't pester each other. Whenever someone is unhappy there, it's not for long, and those who feel well aren't cocky about it.

The people who live where these ideas exist are far removed from finding pleasure in another's displeasure and feeling an odious joy when another is in a quandary. There, they are ashamed by any instance of schadenfreude; they would rather suffer harm themselves than willingly see harm come to another. There, people need beauty, in that they do not enjoy seeing others hurt. Everyone there wishes only the best for everyone else. No one lives there who wants the good only for himself, instead he wants only to know that his own wife and children are in good hands. He also wants the wives and children of others to be happy.

If a person there sees anyone unhappy, then his own happiness is already destroyed, because where charity lives, mankind is a family. There, no one can be happy if not everyone is. Envy and jealousy are unknown and revenge an impossibility. There, no person is in the way of another. No one triumphs over another.

If someone shows signs of weakness for a day, then no one rushes to take advantage of this. Everyone is considerate to one another. There, everyone possesses a similar strength and yields equal power; the strong and the mighty thus can't reap the admiration of others.

Gracefully, without violating reason and understanding, people there take turns giving and receiving. There, love is the most important law, friendship the foremost rule.

There are no rich, no poor. Where healthy people dwell, kings and emperors have never existed. There, the wife doesn't rule over the husband, nor the husband over the wife. Except over one's self, no one rules there.

Everything there serves everything, and clearly there is the universal desire to seek to eliminate pain. No one wants to revel, therefore everyone does. Everyone wants to be poor, thus no one is poor.

There it is beautiful, there I want to live! I want to live among people who, because they restrain themselves, feel they are free; among people who respect one another, among people who know no fear, there I want to live! But I must admit I'm fantasizing.

2.

Once there was a world where everything transpired very slowly. A pleasant, one might say healthy, languor ruled people's lives. To some extent they idled along aimlessly. What they did they did thoughtfully and leisurely. They didn't work themselves inhumanly hard, in no sense did they feel called upon to wear themselves out or work themselves into the ground. Among these people there was no haste, restlessness, or undue alacrity. No one especially exerted themselves, and that's why life was so amiable.

To anyone who has to work hard or in general stays supremely busy, pleasure is vitiated, makes a sullen face, and everything one thinks is joyless and sad.

Idle hands are the devil's workshop, as a hackneyed old saying has it. The people of whom we're speaking here in no way fulfilled this somewhat rude proverb; quite to the contrary, they refuted it and stripped it of any meaning.

Living well on a harmless, trusting earth, they quietly enjoyed an existence of beautiful dreamlike serenity; they completely avoided vice, in so far as the thought of it never crossed their minds. They remained good because they knew no desire to seek distraction; they ate and drank little because they felt no need to gorge.

Boredom, or what we understand by that, was completely unknown to them. Devoting themselves to all sorts of rational considerations, they lived seriously and at the same time cheerfully. Workdays and Sundays they didn't have, each day was the same. Life flowed on like a placid river, to no one did it occur to complain about a lack of enticement or encouragement.

These people lived a life as simple as it was joyful. Their existence was sweet, tender, and sunny. Far removed from the greed for glory, the unhealthy voracity for fame, and vanity, they were shielded from these three terrible maladies; far removed from lovelessness, they knew nothing of this pestilence that plagues human existence.

Like flowers they lived and wilted. No plans of an unrestful, exciting nature troubled or importuned their heads; thus untold suffering remained forever foreign and unknown to them.

They were calm in the face of death, bewailing neither the dead nor themselves too much for their having lost them. As each loved the other, the individual was not excessively loved and the pain of parting wasn't as severe.

Savage love stands beside savage hate, savage desire beside equally savage grief. Where there's reason everything is subdued, everything is gentle, patient, and sensible.

War broke out. Everyone hurried to the assembly points to pick up their weapons. Our worker also hastened there without thinking twice. What was there to consider when it came to serving the Fatherland? Service to the Fatherland dispels all thought.

Soon he stood in the ranks and, as he was strong by nature, found it divinely beautiful to march with his comrades along dusty roads against the enemy. Singing songs, they pushed on, and soon the battle ensued, and who knows, perhaps the worker was amongst those who fell in battle for the Fatherland.

1915

CHAMBER PIECE

I KNOW a writer who, after struggling in vain for weeks to unearth a suitable subject, finally came up with the droll idea to organize an expedition beneath his bed.

The result of this daring and dangerous undertaking was, however, as anyone could have told the one carrying it out, exactly nil.

Disappointed and disheartened, the adventurer had to stand up again from the floor upon which he had thrown himself, keenly regretting that he hadn't discovered any interesting material for an essay worth the slightest mention.

"What am I going to do now, and how, for heaven's sake, am I going to earn my pitiful, meager daily bread in the future?" he asked himself, filled with worry and trepidation.

As he pondered a way out of the spiritual darkness surrounding him, suddenly he saw, right in front of his nose, a strange and fascinating spectacle that from afar he would not have dared hope ever to encounter.

Stuck in the wall, which was gray, black, and moldy, was an old rusty nail from which dangled an umbrella.

"Lo and behold," exclaimed the delighted writer happily and loudly, "that's incredible! Upon my immortal soul, I've found the most contemplative, most beautiful theme."

Without pausing to reflect for even a moment or taking the time to thoroughly scratch his head, which, after all, he liked to do once in a while before repairing to work, he stepped up to his writing desk, sat down, eagerly grasped his pen and swiftly wrote the following:

"I've seen something unheard of, something in its way magnificent.

"I didn't need to go far. The thing was quite near.

"I was standing in my room lost in thought, when suddenly I saw something weary of life hanging from something exhausted by life.

"It was an old, tired nail about ready to fall out of its hole, which no longer properly held it, and from which hung an almost equally old and worn-out umbrella.

"To see how one old and sorrowful thing clung to another old and sorrowful thing, to see and observe how one decrepit thing clung to another decrepit thing, as though they were two beggars embracing in some cold, hopeless wasteland in order to perish, clinging to one another, prepared at any moment to die—

"To see how something weak in its weakness still supported something else weak before it completely collapsed from its powerlessness, and see how the wretched thing in its lamentable wretchedness for so long allowed the other wretched thing to at least keep barely holding on to it, until it itself will have totally broken down—this deeply affected and upset me, and I didn't want to hesitate to record it here."

The writer paused. While he was writing, his hand had grown stiff from the cold, since he didn't have enough money to have the room heated.

Outside on the city streets an icy December wind swept in. For a long while our writer looked mechanically at what he had written, rested his head in his hand, and sighed.

1915

THE COWARD

I HAVE to quickly jot down the peculiar dream I had last night. My heart is quite heavy from it. Perhaps it will be lighter if I write down as precisely as possible what was seen. It concerned a kind of street fight. The street was bright and dusty and glittered in the midday sun. A troop or line of riflemen attacked us with obvious superiority. Oddly, however, I heard no shots. It was more hand-to-hand combat than shooting engagement. Weapons of cold steel, like sabers and scythes, flashed in the sun. We fled—that is, we fell back—because our troop was too small, in order, with a little luck, to offer some resistance. We were split apart and thrown into the nearby alleys. Now, however, came the truly strange, terrifying thing. As for me, I saw myself in the dream as a gigantic fellow, as tall as a lamppost, a magnificent figure of war, bursting with aggressiveness, power, and militant fire; the saber, as God is my witness, I carried in my fist, imagining myself next to invincible. But all at once all my lofty, vibrant, death-defying courage seeped away, and now I began to sink, as it were, step by step. I fell into an unspeakable, sick grief, and minute by minute became sicker. Oh, what agony it is to be timid! Full of shame and fear, I separated from my comrades engaged in combat, cowardly left them to their hard fate and renounced my sacred duty to live or die, stand or fall, triumph or go down with them.

In this moment, when I withdrew from my friends to sneak away into a quiet back alley, I died the most miserable death, and I was soulless. It's the soul that makes us brothers among brothers, human beings among human beings, men among men, friends among friends. Soullessness and heartlessness, weakness, lassitude, and wretchedness coursed through my every limb. I was unspeakably unhappy. Pale and sick, disgraced and dehumanized, I stood there hesitating, while in the still atmosphere of evening the birds sang so beautifully I could have died. The proud, precious saber fell from my limp hand and I let it lie there, and a hopelessness and fear I wasn't able to explain rippled through me from head to foot, drove me into the house. Strangely, however, I remained on the steps as if to examine my behavior one last time. "Coward!" I murmured. Before my eyes stood my tender, precious home, my beautiful wife and sweet children whom I loved above all else. Before my eyes, however, also stood the saber I had thrown away and the battle from which I had fled. Suddenly everything fell into disarray, both what I saw and what I was, and I . . . awoke!

1916

THE SAUSAGE

WHAT AM I thinking about? I'm thinking about a sausage. This is horrifying. Young men, adults, those of you who serve the state, in whom the state puts its hopes, consider me carefully and take me as a stern deterrent, for I have indeed sunk low. I can't tear myself away from the thought of a sausage that I possessed a moment ago and now is gone forever. I pulled it out from the wardrobe and, on this occasion, ate it. With an obviously all-too-sincere pleasure, I consumed what would still be there had I not devoured it. A few minutes ago, the best, juiciest sausage was still there incarnate, but now, alas, due to my all-too-precipitate consumption, the tasty sausage has vanished, rendering me inconsolable. What was still there a moment ago is now gone and no one can ever bring it back. I ate what I never ever should have devoured so quickly, what I never ever should have let myself, alas, smack so hastily. I have gobbled up what I could still have relished had I resisted that craving. I most deeply lament the fact that I didn't resist the craving and that I consumed what minutes ago was still red and fresh and at my disposal but is now no longer and will nevermore be at my disposal because I precipitately disposed of it. I availed myself of what I could now still avail myself of if what occurred hadn't occurred and now can never be made up for again. What is gone could still calmly and peacefully be here, and what has been lost never to be seen again could arouse one's appetite, but the source of the arousal of that appetite is gone, and I truly lament this, although I realize every lamentation is of little or no use at all. What was violated could be unviolated, what was gobbled could be ungobbled, what was snapped up could be unsnapped, had I been more careful and abstemious, but alas I was neither abstemious nor careful and I deeply regret this, although I realize regret and remorse are of little or no use. What has vanished could be here and what's dead could be delightfully alive. What was gruesomely masticated and mauled could be whole, but alas it's been mauled, bemoaning it won't help. What no longer serves could render the best service, and what has been bolted down the hatch could still delight me with its beautiful presence if I had not done this lamentable deed which, alas, I lament for simply too many reasons. What, as I already said, is gone, need not, as I said, be lost, had I been more steadfast and stronger and renounced my wicked tendencies. Terrible cravings, you've robbed me of my sausage. I sampled what, as sample, could henceforth still be sampled had I left it lying there unsampled and unsavored, which, as I've said many times now and can only keep repeating, makes me disconsolate. I brought on defeat by testing an only-too-exquisite sample which now is fully savored and sampled because I wasn't abstemious, which I repent. Repentance is useless, it makes sausage-loss greater rather than smaller, thus I would like to attempt to renounce repentance, which in any case is very difficult because the reason to repent is immense and powerful. I have incurred a defeat because I didn't save what I absolutely should have saved and been careful about, which, alas, I wasn't careful about, though I can hardly believe it, since I was always of the belief that I was strong and resistant, about which, apparently, I'm mistaken, which pains me, although, as I said, remorse is of no use whatsoever. Oh, this sausage, I could swear it was magnificent. It was wonderfully smoked and speckled with enchanting lumps of lard, and it had a thoroughly impressive, acceptable length, and it had a fragrance so mild, so bewitching, and a color so red, so delicate, and it crackled when I masticated it, I keep hearing to this day how it crackled, and it was juicy, juicier than any I'd ever eaten in my entire life, and this juicy and savory item would still be juicy and savory, the redness and delicateness still red and delicate, the redolent still redolent, the exquisite and appetizing still exquisite and appetizing, the longish and cylindrical item still cylindrical and longish, the smoked still smoked, and the speckled-with-lard still lard-speckled, if only I had exercised patience. I would still hear the crackling if it hadn't already been crackled by me, and still have left to bite what I, alas, have all too nimbly bitten to bits.

1917

LAMP, PAPER, AND GLOVES

UNDOUBTEDLY a lamp is a very practical and pretty object. We note standing as well as hanging lamps, spirit as well as gas lamps. When speaking of lamps, lampshades automatically come to mind; that is, they don't absolutely have to. It's not true that they have to. No one forces us to think about them. Hopefully, everybody is free to think what he likes, but all the same it seems the case that lamp and lampshade ideally complement one another. A lampshade without a lamp would be useless and absurd, and a lamp without a lampshade would impress us as unsightly and imperfect. A lamp is there to bestow light. An unlit lamp makes no particularly deep impression. As long as it isn't burning, it's missing its, as it were, innermost essence. Not until it burns does its value clearly come to light, then the sense it possesses radiates and glows most convincingly. It's our duty to pay tribute to and applaud the lamp, for what would we do in the sinister night without lamplight? With the soft glow of lamps, we can read or write as we see fit, and because we are speaking of reading and writing, we think, whether we want to or not, about a book or a letter. Books and letters, however, in turn bring to mind something different, namely, paper.

Paper, as everyone knows, is made from wood and is itself then used for the manufacture of books, which in one respect are sparsely read or not at all, and in another not merely read but veritably devoured by everyone. Paper is so useful that we're compelled and coerced to say: it has an almost phenomenal meaning for advanced mankind. One would hardly err much if one maintained that without paper no civilization whatsoever would be at all possible. What would the arguably, indeed hopefully, more valuable part of humanity do if suddenly paper were no longer procurable or made available? The existence of not only many but an overwhelming majority of people doubtlessly is bound up so fervently with the existence of paper that it terrifies us, because on more or less careful consideration we're hardly able to free ourselves from certain understandable concerns. Generally speaking, there is thick and thin, smooth and rough, coarse and fine, inexpensive and expensive paper and, with the reader's kind permission, several paper types and sorts stand out: writing paper, glass paper, rusted paper, lined paper, wrapping paper, drawing paper, newsprint, and tissue paper. The author's parents were owners of a nice, pretty paper store, thus he's probably able to enumerate like clockwork the various types of paper. By the way, couldn't at any hour—on a narrow slip of paper that we might have seen lying hidden in the dusty corner of a writer's drawer—this story have been written, which reads, roughly, as follows:

ONE WHO NOTICED NOTHING

A short or long time ago there lived someone who noticed nothing. He paid no heed to anything, to him everything was, so to speak, not worth a fig. Perhaps his head was stuffed full of important thoughts? Not in the least! He was completely thoughtless and vacuous. Once, he lost his entire fortune, but he didn't feel it, didn't notice it. It didn't harm him in the least, since whoever notices nothing isn't harmed by anything. If he left his umbrella lying somewhere, he didn't notice it until it was raining and he got wet. If he forgot his hat, he didn't notice it until someone said: "Where is your hat, Herr Binggeli?" He was called Binggeli, but it wasn't his fault that this was his name. He might just as well have been called Liechti. Once, the soles of his shoes fell off and he didn't notice it, went about barefooted until someone called his attention to this obvious peculiarity. Everywhere he was laughed at, but he didn't notice it. His wife went out with whomever she pleased. Binggeli didn't notice anything. He always walked with his head down, not, however, because he was studying. One could steal the ring from his finger, the food from his plate, the hat from his head, the pants and boots from his legs, the coat from his body, the floor from beneath his feet, the cigar from his lips, his own children from before his eyes, and the chair on which he sat, without his noticing anything. One fine day, as he was walking along, his head fell off. It must have not been stuck tightly enough on his neck for it to fall off just like that. Binggeli didn't notice that he no longer had a head, headless he walked on, until someone said, "Your head is missing, Herr Binggeli." But Herr Binggeli couldn't hear what the other said, because, as his head had fallen off, he no longer possessed ears either. Now Herr Binggeli felt nothing more at all, smelled, tasted, heard, saw, and noticed nothing. Do you believe this? If you are good and do believe it, then you'll receive forthwith twenty rappen to buy something nice, yes?

While relating fairy tales, I mustn't forget a pair of gloves I saw elegantly and languidly dangling off the edge of a table. Who might the beautiful, noble woman be who so carelessly left them lying there? They're very fine, almost arm-length, pale-yellow gloves. Such pretty gloves speak powerfully about their owner, and the language is tender and kind, like the conduct of beautiful and good women. How beautifully those gloves are dangling! They smell wonderful! I'm almost tempted to press them to my face, which, of course, might be a bit silly, but how gladly now and then we commit a silliness.

1917

BERTA

BERTA works as a diligent employee in a factory office. By chance I recently learned that her superior—a somewhat elderly gentleman, alas, though quite the gallant, of course—has been acting the part of her lover, coming into contact with her throughout the day. One moment he pretends he's head over heels in love, and the next behaves as if he were her austere lord and master, treating this in every way nice girl with an icy indifference. Is he a cunning devil or someone who just doesn't know what he wants? Today he's an adorer, tomorrow a despiser of the female sex, whichever seems to suit him. Certainly, this gentleman is in no way a singular case, there are more of his kind who act the same or similarly. At any given hour he wants to fulfill her every wish purely out of love and might even want to take her hand, drop to his knees, and kiss it; yet at other times he seems to have recollected himself and deems her no more than a poor little worthless wretch, not worthy of even being fleetingly looked upon with a little kindness and concern. Oh, what a scallywag, what a big shot! Now he's her master, now her servant; now he barks and growls at her in rude, haughty tones; now he pleads for mercy with an imploring look and voice, depending on whatever he deigns to feel like doing. Shouldn't it be considered to one's credit and a necessary duty, for someone in her profession to give the fickle scoundrel a proper poke? Surely hundreds agree with me when I say that such a rotter deserves ten thousand digs in the ribs. Walks with the steps of someone going courting and at the same time with steps of a different sort. Perhaps he's a quadruped? Beats me. All I know is that sometime soon I'll advise Berta to summon up all she can to subjugate this petulant man. Were I a woman, I'd be damned if I submitted to someone like him!

1917

LOUISE

I WAS NINETEEN years old and worked as a sales assistant in Z—.
My friend Paul introduced me to his girlfriend Rosa, who in turn acquainted me with her friend Louise, a kindness that obliged me to be
on my most modest and most polite behavior. Whether or not I really
was always modest and polite then, I don't wish to and shouldn't examine any closer here. With regard to my monthly wages of 125 francs,
I had the impudence to proclaim to myself: "Under no circumstances
does this lummox deserve such a high salary!" At that time, I distinguished myself in the most advantageous—or disadvantageous—manner by the fact that I had extremely little respect for myself but on the
other hand an exaggeratedly high regard for most other people. In this
way we're truly cheeky at nineteen. One lovely day, I no longer know
the exact hour, I dared to write a letter to Louise, whom I revered to
the highest degree, which as far as I can remember began approximately
with the following nifty words: "Dear esteemed Miss, this is the first
time in my young, poor, and possibly completely useless life that I've
presumed to write to a woman, and it cost me much trouble, willpower,
and courage before I ventured to resolve to write the salutation, delighting in being afforded the mere chance to write it." Louise had the
kindness to answer this firstling, in that she posted to me her poetry
manuscript together with an album and the request that the former
be neatly transcribed into the latter in my graceful script. After this
entreaty, could there have been a happier person than the overjoyed
lad to whom the request and petition had been directed? In the finest
hand and with thumping heart I copied the most beautiful and kindest verse, and as I did, I felt I was in paradise. In fact, it takes little to
please a young clerk. In the course of our social relations Louise told

me, in a serious voice, that she found smoking and beer-drinking, which tend to accompany a man's life, loathsome and horrid, with which I wholeheartedly agreed since I admired in advance everything she said. I resolved as firmly as possible and made a profound vow to avoid as much as disdain both of these aforementioned evils, which, however, I by no means had the strength to hold true to at all times and every opportunity, but the mere attempt to be obedient and abstemious delighted me. Ah, beautiful, lost, good times, how you enchant me!

"Nineteen, and still nothing yet done to achieve immortality!" a youthfully bright and at the same time accusatory voice called out inside me. My reading was Lenau, Heine, Börne, and the noble Friedrich Schiller; the latter, by the way, I should never cease revering to the highest. Since I was convinced and imbued with the conviction as deeply as possible that it was definitely high time to dedicate myself to humanity, I wrote to a respected person in publishing that it was my ardent and fervent wish to selflessly and eagerly serve him and the cause whose representative and emissary he seemed to be. "Youthful and impetuous devotee," the man wrote back rather dryly, "it's not as easy as you seem to think to answer and make sacrifices to this cause, when the encyclopedia *Meyers Konversations-Lexikon* is probably the first and ultimately final authority worth considering. That you are in awe of me I can comprehend and condone, since you have good reason to think me a great man." I was taken aback by this curious letter. "This patrician denier of all things egotistical, this exponent of everything that's altruistic and not vain, must be a singular master," I thought, and the desire to espouse and struggle for the lofty goals and purpose of mankind sank stupefyingly fast and forcefully, and its joyful, fresh colors significantly and visibly faded. All the more emboldened, enlivened, and encouraged, I now made the daring and reckless attempt to penetrate the educated and refined set, which until then I had only admired, marveled at, and worshipped from afar. I rented a room from Frau Professor Krähenbühl and consequently got to know rather quickly the best, most splendid high societies, circles, and associations to such an extent that at times

Louise seemed quite inferior and, as it were, proletarian. What an ungrateful monster I was! But the glamour and glory didn't last long; luckily all the fine manners and all the beautiful, intellectual empty phrases and conversations made me terribly frightened just in time, and so I begged Frau Professor Krähenbühl for the sake of God to allow me to move, because otherwise I feared I would perish miserably. The lady smiled and said she regretted my precipitate departure most vigorously, profoundly, and exceedingly, but of course in no way could impede my freely made decision, naturally wished me all the best and dearest things, and was infinitely pleased that I was inclined, as it appeared, to leave her. What blatant, revolting irony that was! But in my heart I was absolutely overjoyed that I could up and skedaddle out of there.

Now I came to the suburban district where carpenters resided. "Examining myself from top to bottom with a certain amount of care," I said to myself, "it's become immediately clear that I fit in much better in the workers' quarter than in higher society; in other words, I fit in better with the poor than in the villa district." I remember I was heartily glad that I had the courage to speak my mind to myself so openly. To arrive at a healthy insight is, for both the outer as well as the inner person, always a great advantage in regard to convenience. At my place in the carpenters' quarter, now and then I saw in the window across the way a poor lad who smoked a pipe in an incomprehensibly appalling manner that made for a mournful and dreadful sight. The mother of the lad who had become corrupted early, or whoever she might be, beat the boy ruthlessly every day, as I clearly heard and observed, and the most dreadful thing about the abuse was the dull indifference with which the boy accepted his wretched fate and that he no longer cried from the blows he was dealt. The woman who struck the boy, the boy resembling a youthful wraith smoking and staring regularly out the window as if he were an old man, his early, horrible affectlessness, the hussy's ferocity, her bright-red nose whose appearance bespoke a deplorable vice: all this produced an image whose hideousness made me shudder. Perhaps I might take this opportunity to observe quite seriously that even though I persistently give preference to beautiful and joyful memories over sorrowful and lamentable ones, for the sake of uprightness, justice, and honesty—qualities which fortunately I do not entirely lack—I must not conceal the evil and wickedness I beheld here and there, because otherwise the honor of my thoughts would suffer. Also, I must venture to presume that for the sympathetic, gracious reader the importance of pain and grief is not less than that of pleasure and smiles. Moreover, I hurt no one when I describe a boy's suffering.

I've all but lost sight of the real subject here, and I now return to it, that is, to Louise. I owe to this kind woman, this "proletarian," such a debt of gratitude, which I'll have to explain in a few short sentences. What a free, brilliant thinker she was, what a large, liberal, kind heart. When I think of Louise it's not so much in a physical way, but instead as something like a pure human soul, and this is certainly significant, since this is the portrait of a woman. Louise was beautiful! But obviously ten thousand times more beautiful than her beauty were her qualities. In the life that has followed, I've hardly ever again encountered such a cheerful and happy woman. She possessed a combination of education and serenity, beauty and joy, of seriousness and kindness which, after all I've seen and experienced in the wide world, I have to call precious and most rare. How many sullen, petulant, and resentful women I've known! From Louise there always emanated a uniform, bright, fresh cheerfulness and contentment. Her intellect and beauty were of equal measure, her spirit and kindness equally considerable. How often it happened that I saw women who mainly had in mind to aggravate themselves and others! Louise was never angry. Her beauty, reminiscent of the moonlit beauty of a medieval Madonna, was little noticed by its owner and bearer. Now and then her lovely hair possessed a certain golden radiance. In her eyes lay kindness and a world of benevolence, yet calm and gentle superiority were no less a part of her. I've seen proud and beautiful women with anxiety flickering in their eyes, worrying that their beauty might fade and their star thus sink. I never witnessed anything like that in Louise. I have seen women pretty as a picture become angry at the wind and the rain that dared cause disorder in the holy sanctuary of their hair, and perhaps I have had the opportunity to observe women clacking their teeth in anger at the new allure of a fellow female creature. We may not be altogether wrong, but we're surely lacking in politeness and courtesy when we dare say that the outward appearance of such women is due to the constant torment they inflict on themselves by a lamentable incessant anxiety about their mouth, cheeks, eyes, hair, and figure. It seems there are numerous women who have never been able to progress beyond the small and basically quite paltry concern with their appearance and can't be happy because they are tormented slaves who tremble before the whip of the pitiful question, "How do I look?" or, "What kind of impression am I making?"

With regard to Rosa, whom I mentioned at the beginning, having introduced her into the company of the worthy reader, I must now concern myself with her, at least to the extent that I don't leave her dangling in just any corner. Paul, her friend and confidant, whom I've also previously mentioned, in time began showing toward his girlfriend signs of his lovelessness and unfaithfulness, which made Rosa cry as well as outraged her, since she was bound to feel the growing indifference and thoughtlessness of her dear beloved as the deepest insult. One day, as I was sitting alone with her in her room, she asked me with, as it were, a dark mien, that is, she requested, or even better, demanded that, in a few words, I tell her honestly and frankly everything I knew about Paul's behavior. "He's your pal," she added. Without a moment's doubt what I should answer, I remarked and replied that because Paul was my friend I had silently forbidden myself at just this moment to have an opinion about him. Believing myself entitled to explain that such confidential revelations and illumination couldn't be of the least value to Rosa, I took the liberty of trying to make her understand in a very simple manner and explain to her as concisely as possible that the opening of an information bureau and the intentions and discretion of an honest man perhaps did not at all correspond. She exclaimed, "Paul is deceiving me, you know something about it, but don't want to tell me—you're abominable!" I remained serenely seated, exhibiting complete calm, and spoke not a syllable. After a few minutes I had the honor, satisfaction, and pleasure of being told by Rosa that I was right. She gave me her hand and was satisfied with me. It generally can be said of Rosa that, by virtue of her kitten-like suppleness and agility, she would have made a superb chambermaid for a great lady, or a dancer at the Royal Opera. She was quite graceful, vibrant, and exceedingly clever. She often used to dance in her room with castanets like a Spanish seductress. She would have probably made a successful actress as well. Even more, I enjoyed envisioning her as a pastoral lass, a shepherdess, or a huntress in the forest, or in a fluttering fantasy costume on an open green meadow. She had wit, grace, and mischief, and with these gifts recalled the rococo period. Nonetheless, later she married a teacher.

For a time both friends were sharing a modest apartment, and Rosa, as well as Louise, had given me permission to come by and knock whenever I wanted, and I did, since dropping in on two lively and clever women obviously made for the greatest pleasure, and moreover I was in store for the special delight, if I may note, that I would be welcomed gladly, and thus I took advantage to my heart's content of the above-mentioned permission, and our meetings were forever cheerful, pleasant, and unconstrained. Louise was always calmness itself. Rosa could, at times, be quite infuriated or depressed. Once, she had seen a man run over by a streetcar. Being utterly aghast at the regrettable incident, almost fainting, being thus agitated, drained, and distressed by what she had witnessed, was by all means becoming to the tender and easily moved Rosa. Louise was, as it were, the large soul, Rosa the sensitive one. In any case, how happy I was at a time when a still-unknown world was opening before the eyes of the inexperienced young man, essentially still too inept and uncultured to enter or travel in it, to be with a circle of acquaintances that allowed me, while I chattered happily and kept them company, to educate myself in various things for free and for my benefit. Education and enthusiastic inquiry were joined most desirably by an amusing, invigorating social intercourse. Lively prattle in their lovely presence was all the young women accepted from me as thanks, so the only tribute I paid them was my young, stupid, satisfied face, apart from my still unpolished manners. I profited from our native Swiss connection, from the advice, lessons, social gratification, refinement, encouragement, and improvement, while I only had to assume the easy obligation not to be totally vapid, dull, and dry, but in every way possible the opposite, strike up a few amiable conversations, now and then laugh loud and clear, kindle the same in my dear benevolent friends, carelessly mix up smart and silly things, in the main be to some extent reasonable and wise, above all to show myself free of any ill humor, evince plenty of wit, manifest goodwill, which has always been essential when it comes to effecting distraction and diversion, and, all in all, prove to the ladies that I was still, yes, a young man. Louise! I need only quietly utter this name—which today, after so many years have passed, has the significance of a monument—to see myself heartened and put in the gayest mood. When, gradually, much or, in God's name, everything becomes lost to the one aging, when he becomes constantly poorer and poorer and everything beautiful and kind crumbles off him and shatters and relentless winds rob him of hope, and when it becomes colder and colder about his head and heart, slowly, as he fears, the joy of living dies in him, unpleasant, frosty suppositions inevitably turn into facts—a likely most dismal and unpleasant reality—still the memories come, the again and again new, fresh, warm, youthful remembrance of diminished and vanished lovely times is at least not lost to him, and we shouldn't be surprised to witness him caring eagerly and conscientiously for this memory, because, beautiful in and of itself, it alone affords the one whose life has grown poor in beauty and joyful hours more beautiful, joyful, and pleasant hours. He knows why he so diligently endeavors to prevent the destruction and disintegration of his lovely, joyful Jerusalem, he knows why he so faithfully and persistently sprinkles, sprays, tends, and cares for the dear garden of his memory and why he makes it his assiduous duty to plant and place the blossoming, living past in the cold, naked present.

Louise, the daughter of an honest rural carpenter, came early to the city to seek work, where she found a position with a Mr. Mortimer. Angelic beauty that she was, she soon had her master at her feet, who adored his worker and subordinate passionately. With her wondrous and soulful eyes, she looked at him gently and listened, smiling, to his ardent assurances. The fact that she was superior in every way—in wit, intelligence, intellect, spirit, and taste—to her manager and employer did not prevent the noble, beautiful soul from succumbing and giving in to his tempestuous, domineering desire and accepting all the unreasonable demands of his powerful longing. She surrendered to him, that is, she allowed him to do whatever the rapture her presence instilled in him commanded. She shivered from the effect of his kisses. Since she had once fancied being a maid, a servant, an obedient slave, she was blissful, and the boldness of the thought of being of boundless service and amenable to her master thrilled her to her core. Was Mr. Mortimer indifferently gifted? So it seems. He was handsome and vain. About the considerable amount of self-love that literally enfragranced his person, even those who had observed him only fleetingly could be in no doubt. As for the rest, we'll try to avoid judging him all too harshly, since doing so would wrong him. Yet he did, after all, seem to belong to those men who are adept at sufficiently imbuing themselves in the most advantageous manner with their astonishingly elevated sense of worth. Here, however, we are dealing with a flaw or vice that lovers perhaps love above all else about the object of their affection. If, on closer inspection, the beautiful proletarian would not have held the rich, proud, powerful business magnate in high esteem, it must be said she would have loved him all the more. Love has very little, or in general not the least, to do with appreciation and respect. Love does not inquire as to whether the beloved is worthy of deep respect. If I'm not mistaken, Mr. Mortimer was something of a Freemason. Louise introduced me to him one day, but as far as I recall the two of us exchanged only a few and, moreover, quite meaningless and dry words. He made as little impression of intellectual acumen as of toughness. When I saw him, I took him immediately for a hedonist and weakling, for a bon vivant with an epicurean nature who delighted in devouring, consuming, and greedily gobbling up everything feminine and complaisant that drew near him. Perhaps you find I'm handling Mr. Mortimer too roughly, and I willingly confess that unfortunately this might be the case. I only harm myself by this. Some men are ordained to be of great value, especially to women, yet as contemporaries and fellow creatures they sometimes possess, as if providence and heaven saw to a proportionate distribution of gifts, little or not the slightest significance; apart from love-related issues, they are of no importance, and as a driving force in matters of state or human affairs, they rate no consideration. Enough! Louise, the noble one, was, in any case, the debased beloved of this seemingly quite weighty, significant man, this imposing representative of all things smug and holier-than-thou. Mortimer was married. Louise, however, to my knowledge was never in any contact with Mrs. Mortimer. There was, then, no relationship or communication between the two women, for which, after all, surely there was not the least reason. When Louise became the mother of a son, the lioness, the heroine within stirred and Mortimer was bade farewell. On that occasion, filled with unmistakable majesty, endowed with gentle yet unshakable resolve, she told him that in the future she wanted to be alone, that she no longer wished to see him, that her desire was for him to keep his distance from her, that in her inmost being she had broken with what had been and occurred. He offered her further financial support. "None of that. Go," she said cuttingly and calmly, whereupon she showed him eyes full of dismissal and indifference. She hardly seemed to recognize him any longer, he was a stranger to her. When he beseeched her to have pity on him, she bade him, in a cold and formal way that terrified him, to remove himself, whereupon he left.

Louise now began to struggle with the hardships and exigencies of everyday life, a battle that was just as hard as it was cheerful, frank, and fearless. When I saw her in her uncertain condition, she seemed every time just as poor as she did courageous, just as needy as she did smart, brave, and happy. I have seen her in the poorest situation and in the most miserable circumstances, but I always found her willing to speak gaily, to show grace and spirit, and to smile happily and confidently. Always she remained calm and composed, and for the little gaieties that keep your chin up, she demonstrated a constant, charming, and delightful understanding. Such a woman, such a stout character, may and must prevail. And, indeed, in the end she was victorious in the hard battle, defying all the hostile storms and forging ahead through all the difficulties. In the war of everyday life, she became strong and never forgot to laugh, communicate, and be kind. To a high or the highest degree, poor herself, she was a constant, true friend to others who were poor. She lived as a proletarian among proletarians. She rose, we might say, to be the beloved and admired queen of the indigent. By heartening and consoling others, she heartened and consoled herself again and again. Of exhaustion and completely losing heart Louise knew nothing. —Is she still alive? And if so, where does she live? It's already been a long, long time since I last saw her. Life tore me away from her neighborhood, away from the company of the excellent one. Of course, I would like to see this treasure once more, and it may well come to pass that we will meet again. In the past I, too, had left her for a while, but I remember I was always drawn back to her again as if to a beautiful, propitious star.

1917

RAIN

THERE'S gentle but also unruly rain. We prefer the former but take it as it comes. To accept what comes and yet never lose one's cheerfulness isn't easy, but is beautiful because of that. What tastes the sweetest? Natural honey? No, something else: peaceful, everyday work without calamity. Speaking of rain, you could say it makes the earth black and soddens the streets. I deeply hope more will occur to me. Dark rain clouds have something cozy, poetic about them. Is that it? Oh no, Mr. Author! I request a smidgen of patience so I may collect myself. Sentences, words don't just fly to me, they want to be caught unawares, captured, attained, discovered, enticed. Sometimes the mind thinks more about zwieback than about language and the like. In general, we have spring rain, autumn rain, etc. Rain is wet. That has been the case and we assume will remain so. No one should ever succumb to the opinion that he is unique. We're all like one another, at least I firmly believe this, and furthermore I believe everything has already happened and existed once before and that's why all pride seems exceedingly superfluous and inexpedient.

But why, dear friend, don't you stick meticulously to your drizzling theme? In fact, often it only drizzles. But more often it pours and rains in real torrents, as if it wanted to inundate every path, park, dear, lovely garden, every field and the paraphernalia hanging there. To be drenched by rain now and then isn't at all funny, rather it can be quite irksome, which without doubt everyone will have experienced in his dull or eventful life. In a proper rain everything becomes wet except water, like rivers, which can't possibly get wet because they already are. What I am I can't become, and what I have can't be given to me. Rain moistens roofs, fills holes and barrels with water, swims and runs down slopes, washes useless stuff away, sees to it that everything all about glitters watery, swallows up and gulps down dust, is a sweeper and wiper who diligently wipes and valiantly sweeps up and makes those who don't carry an umbrella scurry along. How richly thinged the world is; again and again we sincerely have to adore it. Should it also be permitted to think about excursions, entire cities, wide verdant landscapes filled with fruitfulness, of Russian, Bavarian, Belgian, Thuringian, North American, Spanish, Tuscan regions moistened and injected with abundant wetness? Or about historical pageants, the dense crowd breaking up, seeking shelter that looks quite pleasant? Wouldn't a dreamy poet in rainy weather like to sit at a dear old window so as to feel inordinately lonely? If I'm not mistaken, it rained endlessly, as it were, during the Battle of Dresden and Napoleon got thoroughly soaked.

Many years ago, as it dripped and rained enchantingly, I promenaded and strolled along the local Bahnhofstrasse which had duplicated itself, its facades, trees, gentlemen and ladies, primarily these, boys and girls and kittens and I don't know what all, magically reflected in the smooth asphalt and in the soft afternoon light in such a way that there was an upper world and a lower world and the unfathomable seemed almost more beautiful than the real. Desist, desist. Relent and break off. Consider whether this article perhaps isn't already almost too grand and difficult.

1918

PENCIL NOTE

"ABOVE all, within the scope of our capacities, it's necessary to combat anarchy. The danger lies in wait for us from within. All bad things lie within our unfortunate condition, within our evil composition. There's probably no fear as justified as the fear of yourself. Fear nothing as strongly as your insincerity.

"It's almost boring that it's always the simplest things that are urgently in need of being said. The simplest thing is for most people much too—simple! They disdain it and thereby also their most important vital interests. Simplicity doesn't fawn upon us; thus we want nothing to do with it. One thing flatters the other, until it shows its claws and out of anger they crunch each other with their teeth or tear each other apart or scratch out each other's eyes.

"You have to wangle the funny out of the fiend and laugh at it. Perhaps the evil will feel ashamed and become better. Better? Ah, there's the catch! To change is uncomfortable and to improve—insulting.

"Where should I place this article? I'll title it 'Pencil Note.' Perhaps the *Peruvian Evening Post* or some flyer will accept and print it.

"It could also be that I'll tear up what I've written and throw it out the window since I'm not at all keen on publication."

The poet lit a match and burnt the sketch, just as witches and heretics were burnt in the past, which, thank God, has long since gone out of fashion.

"Today, we're merely put under arrest as politely as possible. All kinds of instruments of torture hang in historical museums, for example in Nuremberg, where they preserve tongs but fortunately not the pinching.

"The embers used in pinching off fingers have gone out. Another and more beautiful glow lives on, and there is a fire that can never sputter and die, whose flames, though invisible, shine from souls that burn with a noble fervor.

"Now I'm going to smoke a cigarette and think about a small town."

1919

LETTER FROM BIEL

WITH THE apples you sent me, a true autumn has flown into the house. I want to set them aside and for the present simply satiate myself with my eyes! To bite into such beautiful fruits would be a sin and a shame.

You've already delighted me often with amenities. Where did you get such a talent for such sweet surprises? Your generosity almost crushes me. You're always the noble giver and I the endlessly taking, ignoble recipient.

Perhaps I can at least show you a sign of my gratitude by giving you my new book, as soon as it appears in print. Until then, of course, time and tide will still slip by.

May I assume you are well? You're always well, because you have a patient temperament and calmly discharge your daily duties.

So, you're called Frieda.* Up until now I erroneously took you for a Flora. You've always signed your name only with an F. Frieda is a name that undoubtedly suits you, because you are pacific and soft. I shall commit it to memory once and for all.

Recently I saw a pretty young girl running off like a deer. Youth is something magnificent, but it has the disadvantage that from day to day it grows older, while riper years have the advantage that inwardly they become rejuvenated. Surely you won't take it amiss that I also look at and find adorable others besides yourself.

---

*As Jochen Greven's note in the *Sämtliche Werke* informs us, a few individual sentences from this story (four by my count) derive from Walser's December 6, 1918 letter to Frieda Mermet (1877–1969), director of laundry services in Bellelay, where Walser's sister Lisa was a schoolteacher. *Friede* is peace, tranquility, quietude.

Biel, with its charming surroundings, always reinvigorates me. Although I have more to do than I would prefer, every day I climb up the mountain a good distance in order to breathe the fresh air. With a few steps you're already in the middle of forest and field, that is, in a countryside no one regards as highly as a writer who sits for hours at a time at his writing or study desk, where now and then he sighs because he longs to be in motion.

Yes, our lake country is beautiful, life here is good, I sense this with gratitude. The region is open and free and everywhere offers an enchanting view. Walking and strolling about here is glorious in every direction. The paths have something secretive, endearing about them.

Lake country augurs a lake, and on the lake there may be an island named the Petersinsel, which is dreamily beautiful, especially in the spring when it's like a fairy tale lying on the water. Would you like to see it sometime? I'm certain you would be delighted. Wine can be drunk there and fish eaten, if desired.

Biel seems to me as rich in commerce as in nature. The location is extremely favorable. To the north lies the Jura with beech and fir forests. There you find Delsberg and Pruntrut. Walking south you come to Bern and Thun, to the Alps. Westward is Neuenburg, eastward Solothurn, whereby it occurs to me that we'll want to march over the Weissenstein, you in ladies' shoes, I in soldiers' boots. The plan is ready, only the fulfillment leaves something to be desired. But what isn't yet may still be.

Old landmarks hidden here and there tell silently but clearly that Biel once belonged less to the Byzantine Empire than to the Prince-Bishopric of Basel.

Mett, Brügg, Port, Madretsch, Jens, and Bözingen are some of the villages that lie nearby. To attempt to enumerate them all would be to become lost in prolixity.

I could report briefly on two outings, one that directed me to Aarberg, the other to Büren, two delightful small towns distinguished by a castle, a church, and a bridge. In each town I found it suitable to drink a glass of wine. Both times the sun shone pleasantly.

Büren has a brickworks, Aarberg a sugar factory. Both villages, although architecturally different, are equally charming and look like tranquility personified lying in the lowlands that once may have been covered with ocean or lake water.

Here, one wants to give the impression of being geographically well versed. With everything subject to error, caution seems advised.

In Aarberg, a firefighting exercise was taking place, and with the valiant men jumping about with hoses and around fire engines, it was a pleasure to play the spectator. Aarberg has only one, albeit wide, alley, which looks like a market square. I must talk especially about the bridge. It's a magnificent construction originating in the Renaissance. Alas, I've forgotten the year as well as the name of the architect. Anyone who steps onto this bridge and isn't unreceptive to architecture has to either shout for joy or at least laugh quietly to himself. There's hardly anything elsewhere in architecture as sturdy and at the same time as graceful.

In Büren, the coffee shop delighted me. When I praised it aloud, the proprietress said that for Büren the place was good enough. I responded that I was convinced that with such a nice room one could reap honor anywhere, as much as one wanted, even in the largest and finest cities.

Recently I was told how beautiful it is on Lake Geneva. How rich our homeland is in scenic beauty. I don't doubt that it's glorious to be a citizen of this country and to contribute as much as possible to its prosperity. You, my worthy fellow citizen, are warm and kind and representative of something robust.

I would be surprised if the times in which we live were not favorable to women. In the Middle Ages, Bertha reigned over Burgundy, and from what we know from books, she diligently saw to the dissemination of culture and education by building countless churches, though not with her own hands—she had laborers erect them.

Every humble woman can be a kind of queen in her domain and make herself useful in her narrow circle by governing sensibly. It is for all of us important that we discover our essence and allow the degree and peculiarity of our powers to take effect.

I hope it snows vigorously this winter. Isn't that your wish as well? Snow is so beautiful. You love it, too, don't you?

1919

THE FIRST POEM

HE STOOD stock-still, simply looking around him. Was he writing a poem? Indeed, he had come here to produce his first poem. Because he had hurried here to do so, he was already warmed up.

And now he was partly excited, partly afraid. Excited because he wanted to create, afraid because he thought he might fail.

Although still young, he had struggled ardently for some time. Already he had written quite a lot of useless junk, that is, composed verse that seemed to him deficient. Publishers didn't have to fear he would submit any of his manuscripts to them for evaluation. Fortunately, up to now he had thought only slightly about publishing. He was keenly aware that he wasn't at all qualified yet for the book business. He was more devoted and wistful than recognized, more budding than famous.

From his coat pocket he now pulled out his notebook or diary. A suitable pencil was already sharpened, and now he could start to formulate and at any moment begin composing.

And this he did. A biting wind whistled through his thin suit, a sort of tuxedo. The dance began.

He was wonderfully suffused with a love for his work, with bravery and the claims of art, and finally with risibility. Because he stood there so patiently, of course he had to laugh out loud at himself.

"How comical I am," he exclaimed, "eavesdropping on Nature." There wasn't that much special here to hearken to. Everything around him was scant of sound. Now and then there was only a cry of, perhaps, a fox. Probably few others would stand there thus deprived and bear what he, the one pursuing the art of rhyme, bore.

When I say he laughed, that's based on fact, and when on the other hand I say that nevertheless he was serious, this is no less true. He stood here out in the open as in a temple, considering, and breathing many times into his numb hands.

At home, before he took off, he had rubbed his limbs vigorously, which he regularly and gladly did, since it was like a religious exercise. Religion was immense and sweet, one was much like the other, each in its own way.

It pleased him that he stood in hardship as in a spiritual fire. The thought that everything beautiful and good is difficult instilled comfort in him. Nearby a leaf trembled in the wind. He incorporated this into his poem, as well as a tousled tree, a little heap of snow that lay in a ditch, even himself who one day would be lying on the ground like the leaf and the lump of snow.

Part of the forest appeared leafless but still warm and pleasant enough. Round about lay mountains, and before no matter what door or beside some hedge there stood a poor person. No one escaped hardship.

In poverty lay a joyful sprightliness and freedom. The cold kindled incandescence. Whoever never faced uncertainty or never suffered anything or never trembled because of something held dear knew little about happiness, and whoever was always victorious was never truly a victor.

He jumped back and forth along the hillside a few times, which looked a little foolish. Below lay the gray city delicately reminding one of spring.

"Is someone crying?" he asked. He had the impression that somebody was turning their face to hide their tears. Now he incorporated the face into the poem together with the mountain peaks, as well as all the world's grieving, hoping it would be suitable to be taken seriously by sophisticates and give to friendly folks a little joy.

No one disturbed him because at the moment most people preferred to be at home sitting in their warm rooms rather than walking in the freezing cold.

At last he was finished. He titled the poem "Little Landscape." At home he would write out a fair copy, so that, perhaps, he could send it soon to a woman who would take pleasure in the modest gift.

Because night had started to fall, he went home. He was happy like never before. Outwardly he was the same, and no one remarked how overjoyed he was about his first poem.

1919

THE COMRADE

IN ANY case, I was going through some strange times then. Perhaps, though, I can relate something ridiculous here. I lived in a small town, about which I was as happy as a child. A little country town with castle towers and a wall had always been my dream. The job was quite pleasant; the people treated me amicably. Still, I was dissatisfied and almost perished from anxiety. The new place was to my liking and at the same time unbearable. How could that be? What was to blame for this reprehensible perplexity?

I had dreamt this up damn beautifully and now it was null and void. Everything around me seemed trivial and foolish. Did that arise from within myself or from somewhere outside me? Heaven only knows. Suddenly everything within and without was worthless, which, of course, tormented me greatly. What oppressed, bore down on me? Had I lost money? As if at that time I would have thought about money in any way!

No, it was about something much more stupid. However, since I took it very seriously there was nothing at all dumb about it, yet nonetheless it was incredibly dumb.

The best thing I had going at that time was a pal my age who wrote me a letter in which he confided that he loved a woman. For me that was something stupendous, and from that point on I was displeased with myself.

In my overhastiness there was nothing more urgent to do than thoroughly denigrate myself, which was obviously inappropriate. But I was young and tempestuous, and about the value of compromise I knew nothing.

The thing was that up to now I had foolishly thought it impossible for something so grand and lofty to befall either of us. The two of us were indeed much too poor and awkward, above all much too insignificant, for that to happen. Without question he and I were much too crude, etc., to have a sweetheart.

Before, of course, I had always waited anxiously, so to speak, for something curious to occur, and yet always smiled thinking it never would.

Now it came after all. My pal had a love, and what an earnest, deep one! Apparently, he had become a totally new person, a lot more outstanding, and in the briefest time, as if from one day to the next. Compared to him, what then was I?

For days I chewed over the letter, which sounded strangely serious, and I fell kind of ill from it. At first nothing pleased me anymore. Today I laugh because I find it all droll. At that time though, I was in a state, and of laughter there was not a trace.

What I had never before experienced I now experienced. What I had never before seen was now visible. Like a giant the experience stood before me. Rather, it wasn't I who experienced it, but he did, and I experienced it with him. Had I felt it in my own person, perhaps it would have affected me less strongly. It was wondrous. It was like an incomprehensible noise in the night, an impenetrable forest, an unexpected torrent. In short, it overwhelmed me.

Because my comrade loved a woman, I couldn't sleep at all, or only sparsely and poorly, which was extremely hard on me. I had little or no interest anymore in food, drink, entertainment, or my daily affairs. This wasn't right! Because of him I took the liberty of exposing everything around me to an unjustified condemnation that verged on contempt. What rashness!

I saw him as a huge, happy person striding over a mountain range, his head raised high, his hair free in the storm that shook the trees. His zest for life compelled him to laugh out loud. "How the brave one must be developing all his talents now so that he hardly knows fatigue any longer! How splendid his indefatigability!"

At home, in my nice but musty room, despondent, I wrote on a sheet of paper: "Why am I, poor and small, dwindling away, and so dispirited that my heart leaps as if it wanted to kill me? How hideous dejection is. Love uplifts him, me it oppresses. He walks joyfully, I sorrowfully. He's doing well, and I'm doing lousily."

I crawled back and forth as though in a fever. Bright sunshine infused me with cold and a whirling vertigo. And I lost all my perseverance, an indication of good health, and imprudently proceeded to insult my boss, whereupon I was in for the pleasure of hearing that I was free as the wind, that is, fired.

And to top it off, all of this happened mainly because my comrade loved a woman. Was I nuts? Oh no, not at all! I was in a battle with myself and eventually was heartily glad to run away.

Many old people find life uncommonly comfortable. The young, with their peculiarities and youthful blood, insist on making it harder on themselves than many precipitately think. We can be jovial and at the same time unhappy; on the other hand, we can be morose while secretly being immensely amused. With a little more mindfulness, all kinds of mistakes regarding this matter could be brought to light.

1919

THE PROLETARIAN

A YOUNG proletarian said to me: I go to work every day, we're called workers, nothing else, but something's missing. The question is, in what sense do we work?

After work I stand around and look at the people and have thoughts that come of their own accord, I don't want them, but all of a sudden there they are and they interest me. This comes and goes. I can't imagine anyone who doesn't think. Surely everyone does that.

My buddy fell in battle, he went into it with an indescribable ardor I didn't understand. Compared to him I'm a child. He was untamed and I loved him because of his vigorous nature. Now he's gone, and what do I, the one living, desire? Why do I live?

At times it seems to me that all the good ones are dead and nothing beautiful is left, but that's only my moods. Aren't I often discouraged but soon happily back to laughing and joking again? There're such nice girls around; they have funny faces and talk so comically.

I don't like to politicize, that seems dull to me. I want to work and other than that just try to amuse myself. I take the world as it is. Busy hands seem more important to me than incoherent chatter.

Politics is an art, and the simple man does best not to concern himself with it since nothing ever comes of it. People should be honest, guileless, and friendly, and that's what I want to be, too.

Brooding over what makes sense and trying to depict a worldview, that's something different. I enjoy doing that because it seems beautiful to me. Everything beautiful deserves to exist, whether it be a nice thought or a painting. I'm always looking for something that strikes me as beautiful and can enrich my life, that's what matters.

I seldom read newspapers because I want to make up my own mind; I'd prefer to go for walks where I hear and see things and read from the book of life, which certainly contains excellent articles.

Then I climb up the mountain, lie down on the moss under the wide branches of a fir tree and dream, and perhaps smoke a little, and above me in the distant sky is the infinite, and the sun gilds me lying there, and every thought takes on a luster—how can I say it? In any case, I can do this all afternoon without getting bored, which to me is something completely unknown and I have no wish to learn.

Now and then, yes, it happens that I yearn for more than what life offers me. Then all kinds of things occur to me, countries and oceans, cities. When I see trees, I think: How calm and benevolent they are. Why aren't human beings like that as well?

To love, to work a great deal, to feel so much joy! I hope something divine might stir within us. I never go to church. Doesn't it tempt me? What do I believe in? I don't know, I know only that I miss a lot if I don't believe.

Couldn't faith emerge anew among people? Wouldn't that be a wondrous occurrence? Basically, everyone longs for this, even if they smile as soon as it's imagined. It doesn't seem to have anything to do with concerts, theater, or any kind of learning. Everyone was enlightened a long time ago. What do I get from it? A few things I understand. Well, that's something and nothing.

What people miss is something they can have reverence and respect for. If someone wants to kneel, he doesn't know where; he sees nothing exalted. But perhaps it'll come one day and there'll be something temple-like again, maybe centuries from now.

I also find life beautiful when it's poor. I take delight in getting up and going to bed, in an individual word, a bough in blossom, a beautiful book.

The good never vanishes; something modest always remains with us. The little ones are satisfied with little oddities and do everything to inspirit themselves with insignificant things.

I walked far and wide, wandered astray, and now have arrived at what's simple, tender, and caring. I know better than to expect anything from our pride and greed.

Shall I go and pray or shall I dance? Who's going to tell me? I'm willing to tell myself what's important.

All of us are lonely and want to be connected, all kinds of threads lead us to things that are always the same. Don't we all have something we hold dear, something that engages us, and isn't that enough?

1920

THE AVIATOR

HE LOOKED very fine, that is, manly, strapping. About a year ago an illustrated magazine published a profile of him. I gather that he grew up as the son of a doctor in a small mountain town. Because I was a soldier there, I know the place. The air is splendid, the people friendly, the area uncommonly lovely. Alpine meadows and mountain peaks and ruins of knights' castles all around. How did the boy come to his profession? Well, he would have been propelled into it. One day he flew over the Alps, an incident that made him famous. One read about him in all the capitals. An athlete's fame is perhaps of a somewhat colder kind. It's possible that he sensed this, and that might have cooled him down, dumbfounded him, so to speak. Not every recognition has a deeper value for us. We can be applauded and left indifferent by this. We can come to be recognized and yet all the while constantly feel deprived. His mechanic he paid magnificently, having good reason to do so, entrusting him as he did with his life. What did this life mean? What sense did it possess? But we shouldn't be finicky, shouldn't ask such difficult questions. He lived and did his job just like anyone else. This one bakes bread, another manufactures clothes, the third is engaged in railroad construction or building bridges; he, on the other hand, in front of the gathered crowd, climbed into the apparatus with reckless aplomb to perform, not unlike a dancer, gymnastics. In time he became wealthy, at least what we call wealthy. In reality he lived hand to mouth, since he spent everything, lived quite elegantly, resided in first-class hotels, provided for women, and kept a servant, as is, after all, only fitting for a man of the world. His fiancée worshipped him. When he had the misfortune to plummet, she took her leave of the world. Possibly this wasn't smart, and yet it also might have been the smartest and kindest thing she could do. Undoubtedly, there is a certain grandeur about it, and surely it's sweet when someone who loves follows the one most dear to her into the hereafter. About this everyone has his own opinion. When he flew toward the sun, sailed through the blue ocean of air and saw beneath him the villages, fields, forests, lakes shimmering golden, the flashing ribbons, I mean rivers, and the round hills and the cities with their towering constructions, schoolhouses, hospitals, churches, banks, factories, and courthouses, and curved like a feathered darling of the air in a comfortable swing around the red evening clouds, surveying life, what did he think, what did he feel then? Shouldn't a sense of idealism and grandeur have made him truly happy? He's rumored to have been coarse in conversation and almost a bit too dry and monosyllabic in his dealings with people. Apparently, he only began to live, that is, thaw, the moment he stepped into his plane and made his preparations to pilot it into the heights. Everyone, in fact, is comfortable only in his element, in his profession, so to speak, in his work, that is, his raison d'être. Once, he met a poet who didn't look at all like one, lived like a day laborer, and like a child believed in God. The pilot invited him to take a ride, but the poet declined the invitation. "People such as I," he said, "prefer to live like any other person. The simpler our lives are, the more we're tempted to write." The aviator found the remark comical and went on his way. He couldn't quite understand him. How could he have known, for example, that some of Novalis's character traits were akin to those of Napoleon? Such things and those of a similar nature were unknown to him.

1920

MUNICH

TWENTY years ago, I traveled to Munich and became acquainted with the Dauthendeys, who warmly hosted me. I gave a reading of my manuscript "The Boys," a dialogue piece that, along with three others from those days, is about to be published by Bruno Cassirer in Berlin. They asked me to write something in their album, which I did. It turned out colossally stylish, what with my behaving rather fantastically back then.

With a little stick in hand and a cap on my head I walked in the English Garden and visited Wedekind, who took an interest in my checkered suit. The same cost thirty francs. Suits today are substantially more expensive. For my part I praised Wedekind's green writing desk. With a pleasant smile the author of *Spring Awakening* offered me cigarettes.

A litterateur invited me to a soirée. Among others in attendance was a suffragette who distinguished herself by her short hair and who seemed to me unspeakably wise. She told me that a professor had almost kissed her hand. I recited six of my little stories. Otto Julius Bierbaum nodded approvingly; others, however, found I was taking things too easily. One woman was lying on the sofa like Francisco Goya's *maja*. I took pains to please her; the maneuver proved rather difficult.

The *Insel* magazine was published during that time, and its editorial team lived in a palace where servants stood about here and there and baronesses confidently circulated, which was something fabulous to me. Alfred Walter Heymel seemed the epitome of elegance. Rudolf Alexander Schröder was, first of all, most kind, and second, played the piano extraordinarily gracefully.

I walked into the country and remember seeing villages that, in their toylike diminutiveness, with the church belfry in the center and encircled by hedges, appeared like a thousand years of unchangedness. Also, I made all kinds of acquaintances: here I met with Kubin, there with Marcus Behmer.

Once, there was a studio party. We ate and drank and amused ourselves. Someone showed up as a Tyrolean yodeler, another as a Venetian swordsman. Later, the lights were extinguished and fairy tales were told in the dark. I myself bestowed less attention on the art of narration than on practicing my kissing on the nape of a woman artist who calmly acquiesced to this. What a lovely gaze she had! How nice all this was! I own up to it gladly!

1921

JEAN

JEAN WOULDN'T have been a bad servant, had he had more perseverance. He accepted his obligations effortlessly, as it were, but in general he had no illusions about the duties of his profession. The reason he had become a servant was that there lived in him something that preferred to be concerned with the affairs of others instead of his own. He liked to obey because it suited him. That was Jean. One of his tasks consisted of occasionally brushing the carpets, for which he first climbed up to the terrace and indulged in the beautiful view. Because he was nimble, he could afford to take breaks without attracting the attention of his mistress. This one willfully presented him with an ungracious face to intimidate him, since she was under the impression that he was a bit fresh. Secretly she was quite satisfied with him; for his part, Jean noticed this, thus at least evincing intelligence! Oh, he wasn't stupid and wasn't used to deliberating long. Of the two maids, one was thin and brunette, the other small and blonde. Jean relished the company of these two daughters of Eve and in a short time had ingratiated himself with them. Perhaps this also appertained to his professional duties? That was how he liked to see it. "You should be a bit more forward," they urged him. He didn't need to be told twice, since such a notion had already occurred to him.

The stairs he handled with a soupçon of respect, that is, he lightly swept over them early in the morning; to him it was more a matter of pretty gestures than exactness. He was indeed neat, yet he wasn't prone to exaggeration in this respect. With his master he was occasionally dissatisfied. One day, to bring him over to his side, the master gave him cigars. "Nice of you," Jean said. They stood on the street. The servant immediately lit up one of them. What else could the other person do but put up a brave front before the aplomb the former was displaying? Like all good-natured people, Jean was extremely carefree. Hopefully this virtue will have found the favor of his master and mistress. Once, while serving, he burned his finger soundly and was justifiably proud of his wound. During his off-hours, thinking he would be elsewhere, his mistress caught him lying on the divan reading a classic. "How do you come by such peculiar behavior?" she asked speechlessly, so to speak, to which he responded, "From an innate sense for what's proper. Seeing me here engrossed in one of your books, you can be assured that your servant is of good extraction, which can't possibly displease you." At this the woman laughed, and, since she hadn't done this in a long time, she was in excellent spirits and more satisfied with Jean than ever. He demonstrated a great talent, sensing what might please her, for allowing in only such male or female visitors whom instinct told him she would welcome, but we don't want to depict him as overly splendid. He liked eating honey, by the way, and enjoyed taking walks. Prompted by the latter inclination, he gave up his post. "You would have had a nice life here with me," he was told. "I am obeying higher impulses," he replied, politely bade her farewell, and departed.

1922

THE TWO WRITERS

OF TWO writers, one was uncommonly diligent about his writing but lacked experience. If he had had this, he would have become the greatest of all living authors. Who could doubt it? The second experienced a lot but wrote little, that is, he was shiftless. Indeed, Stendhal was of the opinion that this was only healthy—writing little, that is. While the industrious one found himself in a bit of a quandary about his lack of adventurousness, being reminded of this by the publishers, the other kept busy prattling all day in the society of the vivacious and thus knew little about the battles between literary camps, not to mention writing cramps. To write down his experiences hardly crossed his mind. How capricious the fates are! On some they bestow the irrepressible necessity to communicate, but without seeing to it that they have enough material. Others they endow with imagination while at the same time withholding creative desire.

Now here's how the story goes: The one poor in experience but keen to write approached his counterpart with the polite inquiry as to whether he would be prepared to found a cooperative for the purpose of both writers working amicably together. They came to an agreement and composed with success. The public company prospered splendidly. Diligence now merged with life experience, expressive dexterity with savoir faire. From this arose novellas, novels, and dramas which belonged to the best the age produced, and it produced an abundance, among them good things. If perchance the two writers haven't died in the meantime, they live happily ever after, productive and grinning from ear to ear. Yes, yes, unity is strength.

1922

MUTTERSEELENALLEIN

AMIGO, a reader, couldn't free himself from Alice, who in fact was Helen but was satisfied with the name Alice. Thank you—now, moving on: Who is Alice? A Latin-spouting heroine, living what we call *Mutterseelenallein*, mother's-soul-forsaken, that is, all by her lonesome, upon whom her father bestowed before he died a superb education. For the time being she was living in a hotel; the landlady said to her, "Dear child, with your education, it won't be difficult for you to find a job soon." Reading further, Amigo came to the part in the text where Helen, who consented to the name Alice, found a proper position. In search of a living, she shed pearls, that is, tears, over which Amigo, this paragon of a sympathetic reader, wept. Alice, who found herself placed in a department store, possessed the beauty and behavior of an angel and as such suffered all sorts of hardships. Such things happen, don't they? And now, in gratitude for all that has been read and enjoyed so far, onward! Amigo loved the one he read about; he wished she were real but her description already sufficiently delighted him. Now a female tyrant entered, giving rise to some thrilling scenes. Without her the boss of the company would never have been able to admire Helen, named Alice, for her bearing, and not deny her her recognition but instead offer his devotion by desiring to marry her, which, charmingly bewildered, she declined, because inherent in her was the pretty belief that she would yet obtain another, wherein she was not mistaken. Sweet Alice, ingenuous Amigo. He wolfed down the lines pertaining to her and wanted the book never to end. But how did he ever arrive at this kind of reading and no other?

Constantly her image haunted him; in vain he sought to forget its effect. To his first love he succumbed utterly. We proclaim: What a pity for him, but all the same we wish him our best. There are people who go their own way, and who knows, perhaps he'll emerge a happy man from this story, about which we might mercifully be permitted to smile, if only because of the title.

1923

DON JUAN'S LETTER

I WAS USED to bedazzling hearts. Souls succumbed to me. When I walked along the street, it seemed as if I were clothed in the silk and velvet of lovesick eyes gazing longingly at me. That was certainly a pleasure; I marched and strutted about as if I had been lent wings. I never thought about the consequences of my performance, that seemed immaterial. Had someone wished to draw them to my attention, I would have laughed. Not that I would have become "pious" even today. Piety? I want to pass over that. Don Juan, where's your previous poise, the sheen, the shimmer of your manners with which you did your ravishing? When I set the champagne flute to my lips, from which wit and derisory remarks slipped forth, I was entrancing. You wouldn't believe the things that occurred to me back then, and now what occurs to me is to love you. For me this is completely new. Can you imagine I believe in you as I would in an angel? I don't want to say "angelic savior" because that might ring of pietism. Do I really need to be saved? Still, I would find it charming to be "converted" by you, to be set right by you. Actually, that already happened just from your appearance: I was converted from the moment I saw you. Shall I speak of repentance? Absolve me from that. Let it suffice to hear that, first, I revere you; second, almost worship you; third, have made you my inner vade mecum; fourth, am determined to deliver myself to you, if you wouldn't find that harmful. I'm not really as bad as I myself thought, yet at the same time I'm worse than I was able to perceive. We see ourselves as either worse or better than we are. To penetrate the real is difficult because each of us is a kind of poet who camouflages and conceals. Poetry is both a friend and foe to everyone. I want to marry you, if you'll have me; but if you'd rather leave me unmarried, I'll still be pleased, for I love you and am here to serve you. For a Don Juan to say this, that's saying something; he must be more deeply convinced of the urgency of honest desires for those whom he has taken perfunctorily than other men who have revered and taken them seriously. I used to disregard and take pleasure as I saw fit, now I like to respect and abjure; of course, I don't do this without laughing, which in a sense I let drop down into my Don Juanish self-regard, where it seems nicely kept. Perhaps you're pleased by this letter, which contains a confession without being too humble. The one who kissed Elvira and walked out on her and was up to such delightful mischief can't underestimate himself, by which I mean to suggest that it's not a nobody elevating you to heaven and flattering you with such tenderness that you would have to be pitied were the above not sincere. You looked at me with mistrustful eyes, which proved you do have feelings for me. You know me and yet don't know me. You disdain me a little. First, I deem this rather droll, and second, I agree with you about it, since I, too, in addition to the high regard I have for myself, despise myself a bit. I want to do good, and wish you would welcome this, should you deign to accept me, though nowhere is it written that you must. Though I have always believed in myself, I was never so arrogant as to think I appealed to every woman's taste. If I'm to your taste, take me; if not, then give me the right to go knocking elsewhere. But to gain admittance to you—forgive me if I'm becoming uncharacteristically warm and express a joy worthy of the naive. In the realm of true love, I'm indeed a total novice—in a sense, if you will, young. To me it's as if I've never kissed before. Recently you tried to make me lose my patience. How charmingly you played the indifferent one. Being patient delights me. Is that possible? Have I become someone else? Am I still Don Juan? No, I don't know anything about that anymore. The role is played out. Something has ended and something else is about to begin.

1924

THREE STORIES

Told Based on Book Covers on Display in the Window of a Suburban Bookstore

UNDER THE WHIP OF THE POLISH WOMAN

At one time in a town where the peasantry, as I've been assured, dropped to their knees in droves on the church steps, there was a seemingly, thus not particularly, beautiful woman, but one who possessed the attribute of knowing well how to crack a whip. One might say she had made superb use of an instrument especially effective with the delicately sensitive, for whom a whip in the hand of a woman is something romantic. One knows the appeal popular fare exerts on people in the habit of ingesting the contents of good writing, of so-called high literature, and who have read or, as it were, eaten their fill of a bit too much of it. The woman in question was Polish and, if I'm not mistaken, sat smoking several cigarettes in a bar decorated with delightful drapes while awaiting her guests. Perhaps, then, we find ourselves in Krakow. Once, on commission from a patron, I was supposed to visit one of those districts where landladies exist who are scandalously well attired, but I saw myself clasped by conditions rendering it advisable to decline the invitation. Under the whip of the woman of whom we're speaking, the stateliest members of the male kingdom trembled and yearned, not without an accompanying thrill of joy, and none of them without smiling, when they called on their mistress. Arriving at the Polish woman's establishment, they were eyed up and down so scathingly by her that they almost toppled over from deference, and for all the accommodating and suffering of respectfulness, the standing there stupidly and submissively, and the contempt they could not help but reap, on top of that they had to pay. Circumstances, whence do I summon the courage to spread you out like an expensive Persian rug? What the lane or back alley was called where such things occurred I can't intimate, much less say. A lantern, glittering like a Chinese eye, pierced the fog that might have been there and with its pale rays lured men of great intellect. These are called pillars of civilization. With nothing more than a little rose in her laughing, impertinent mouth, she intimidated them, but one day I read in the morning paper that, against the manipulations of this certainly not ordinary woman, it was deemed appropriate to take steps. At that moment I was engaged with something enticing, with breakfast, and applauded the news.

AMERICAN EDUCATIONAL SYSTEM

How happy this schoolboy was. Perhaps he didn't properly take this into account. Did he already possess enough of a general sense of himself? Do you think he was afraid of his teacher? She sat at her desk with an imperious bearing. She was an enchanting piece of turnery, as thin as a needle. But that's an exaggeration that blushes before us, being confronted with its unpopularity. Concerning the boy's fear, it was his obligation to appear afraid, but inside he was laughing. The teacher's eyes were directed at him with an amazingly sharp and harsh look, but he knew that she was bound by duty to stare at him like this. The funniest, most risible, most beautiful thing was the little paddle she held threateningly in her delicate hand. The little stick in and of itself made fun of this velvet-soft, pale, white, dear, and indulgent hand, and the American lad saw this. At times he stared at the ground, that is, down at the classroom floor, then again at this loveless and yet again so kind face of the instructress. What did the desk think? Nothing? And the boy? He was all feeling. He was supposed to recite something, probably he was really well prepared, but instinctively made believe he was dim-witted, obstinate. He was quite nicely attired. This youngster carried with him into life the impression that to fear something can be to your advantage.

THE PRINCESS AND THE GROOM

In a forest that seemed immeasurable and stretched over sundry hills, accompanied by her hostler, rode for her pleasure the fairest princess a writer has ever fabricated. Obeying a somewhat quaint custom, she wore atop her blondest of blonde hair the blackest, most iniquitous top hat, with a highly elegant ribbon fluttering over her horse's back, as the animal pranced stylishly on the soft ground. Horses feel whom they carry, and ours, too, will have felt its burden in the finest detail. Meanwhile, perhaps, we might disclose, though it's somewhat inappropriate to blab about things like this, that the groom for some time had been gazing at his beautiful mistress with a probably much-too-felicitous mien. Actually, did he know that himself, yet not imagine that knowledge succumbs to feeling and fantasizing because its presence becomes pesky and therefore strikes us as almost ridiculous? Isn't what we shouldn't do sometimes what we most enjoy doing? At this point, they had arrived at a place in the wide, transparent-opaque, heavy, light, misty, bright forest inviting them to stop, which they did.

"How would it be if we alighted here at this adorable spot and rested in the grass?" The princess spoke in the most casual and yet choicest tone of voice. There was nothing left for the groom to do but agree to her wish, for the status alone of the one who had uttered this was enough to command it of him, and so they sat on the ground.

"Ah, the smile," the woman said.

The groom didn't know of whom she was speaking, and because he remained in the dark about this, he sought to at least appear intelligent.

The princess had meant the ground that seemed happy to bear the weight of such a wraithlike body. "I know well that you love me," the reposing one said to the surprised listener receiving her words, "but I hope that your enchantment will never disturb me by even the faintest breath."

The groom's eyes gazed about quite glassily.

"You were born with respect, and thus the more fervently you love me the more it increases, and therefore I trust you. No stammering, if you please."

While dreamily taking a look about into the trees and briefly laughing somewhat shrilly, she gave him unspoken permission to kiss her. He heard what she thought, which of course tormented him. But others also thought of her, because everywhere she went, she allowed their desires to germinate. "I will never need to command you to think twice," she said, stood up and let him help her onto her horse. His composure made him handsome, and she was more beautiful than ever.

1925

THE BEAUTY AND THE FAITHFUL ONE

IN THE salon the beauty, surrounded by gentlemen, sees herself showered with pleasantries. Her paramour seems puny to her; indeed, he sits somewhat to the side, quite meekly but smiling rather brazenly. Does he seek revenge? Rarely has a lover denied having known hatred. The beauty pays him no heed; she is revered, he neglected. Nevertheless, from time to time she looks at him, perhaps with the intention of making him jealous, with the wish to impress him. She's radiant, feels so sure of herself. Must he not envy her, be depressed? To be a minor character out in society: how unbearable!

THE BEAUTY: You've positively vanished this evening; in your unadulterated diffidence you're hardly even visible. No one takes note of you. What are you doing?

THE LOVER (*shows her a lady's handkerchief that he bought from a cabaret artist*): I'm flirting!

The beauty turns pale, flinches, and returns, outwardly calm yet inwardly appalled, to the others; she's disconsolate, feigns contentment. The question "Does he no longer love me?" plagues her more and more by the minute. The certainty of her devotee's being present used to encompass her with an assurance of her beauty. She demanded much from him and believed herself entitled to do so. From no one else did she expect quite such a desire for self-denial, and now this impudence? She sits down, shoots him looks of outrage.

THE LOVER (*to himself*): What won't we do to avoid contempt?

1925

THE ANGEL

AN ANGEL of such kind does well to wait until he's notified that he's needed. Sometimes this takes longer than he anticipates; he, too, simply has to restrain himself and not think he's irreplaceable. I wouldn't want to be the one whom I've made an angel. I deified him so as never to encounter him anywhere again, so that he would be as unalterable as a picture, so that I could gaze upon him according to my needs and wishes and draw courage from the sight. I almost pity him for thinking I was curious and would chase after him, when in fact I have him, as it were, in my pocket, or like a ribbon across my brow. I no longer go to him, am surrounded by his virtue, see myself bathed in his light. Whoever knows how to give, also understands how to take. Both need to be practiced. He arose from compassion, yet it happens that I, the supplicant, play with him. He has doubts, is uneasy. Now I'm faithful, now unfaithful, and he must endure this, the dear one.

1925

CHILDREN AND SMALL HOUSES

RECENTLY it snowed, and so I walked through the town. How lovely it was, how still. All kinds of little imaginings fell from memory into consciousness, like snowflakes floating indefatigably to the ground, which understandably was soft. It was a quite pleasant stroll past cottage gardens and houses, a few of the little houses standing out to me, one with a half-tiled roof. The facade still seemed stately; no, that's not quite right, but its appearance was passable to look at. On one of the cottages was emblazoned the inscription: "If you have peace in your heart, a shack becomes a palace."

A kitten sunned itself on a ledge. Sun? Yes, exactly as I just said, it was snowing and now I'm talking about beautiful weather. Ah, it went like this: As I was strolling along, the sky opened up and above the fallen snow a magnificent blue spread out. A child greeted me and earnestly asked why I didn't have an umbrella. It had, you see, begun to snow again. Is that unlikely? Oh, absolutely not. I responded, "You don't have one either." The child said, "I have a coat instead." "Well, I have one of those, too," I replied.

Again, there were old, small houses along the lane obviously still fit for living and being happy or unhappy in, as the case may be and depending on the circumstances in which their inhabitants lived and breathed. Then along the way came another child; I gave it a coin, and it went happily into a shop to purchase a little bar of chocolate. How dear are small human hands—I almost said: How sweet! Some time ago a woman asked me: "Tell me, what really pleases you? Is there anything that ruffles your cool composure and customary way of thinking?" What kind of a question was that! I was astonished at her manner of trying to intrude on someone's inmost life, and the answer

I gave consisted entirely of a smile. Don't I love some things? But am I always disposed to love? I believe I have the right, from time to time, to be sullen just like anybody. That happens to us all. Had I never hated something, would I have been able to love anything? Joy never ceases, nor does sorrow; I could say more about this, but I don't want to exceed the frame of my little essay that treats of children and small houses, a question in too much of a hurry, the blue sky and the snow. Have you ever caused disappointment in someone and taken pleasure in it? Can we do that? Oh, we can do a lot of things. Yes, many strange things are possible. What lies between this and simple things I'll set aside for now. Nothing of significance shall be said here. Goodbye. Kindness is stupid, but all the same you're likely to have that instinct within you.

1925

GENEVA

FROM BERN to Freiburg by foot takes six hours. In the latter, I bought socks just in case and stroked the little heads of children with the little parcel. On Saturday evenings girls are happy because all the people are walking or standing about intent on shopping, and the next moment doors are, as it were, opening onto the calm and joyfulness of Sunday.

I inquired of a lad about the way to Romont; he stared at my shoes as though he wanted to examine whether they were capable of the journey.

"It's some ways from here," he said.

"Doesn't matter," I replied and in four hours reached the place, ate cheese, drank some wine, and lay down to sleep. Before I shut my eyes, I thought about my sweetheart, which delighted me.

The stretch to Lausanne took eight hours. Perhaps a priest is met on the way there, before whom one raises one's hat, conscious of the fact that it's proper to show a friendly respect for the clergy. This in a high-lying little town called Rue.

Approaching Lausanne, I came face to face with the strolling Sunday crowd. The journey continues and in two hours I'm in Morges whose church strikes me pleasantly and whose establishments seem sublime.

It takes me two more hours to reach Rolle; here, under an awning beside a chestnut seller and a swarm of boys, I roll a cigarette, enter the Tête Noir, an inn dating from 1628, find it clean and respectable.

At eight in the morning I left. Skirting Nyon with its various châteaus, at eleven I reached Coppet, where I treated myself to a salad with meat. The innkeeper, a South American, asked me all sorts of questions.

An elegant woman stood at the buffet; within, I found her a sufficient feast for the eyes for three minutes; she felt it and rubbed her back.

At three in the afternoon I marched into Geneva, proceeded to a café, then come across an old man who lives here with his children and isn't happy about that.

"Disagreements happen," I try to console him. A poster, its writing visible in the distance, reads as follows: BORGIA S'AMUSE. This calls attention to a motion-picture presentation.*

What can one do in Geneva? All kinds of things! For example, you can go into a bakery and ask if you may eat, right there, a bite of sweet pastry to reinvigorate yourself.

Next you can visit the old part of town, look up amazed at churches, and think of Calvin. A marble slab reminds us that the Scot John Knox once preached here.

One can give a schoolchild about to step into a doorway a bar of chocolate, next inspect an art store, bestow honor upon several little pubs, and meet a woman from the Appenzell and ask her where the theater is.

Among the monuments, the statues of General Dufour and the Duke of Brunswick stand out. One monument is to Geneva's entrance into the Swiss Confederation.

You can note museums, splendid private houses, find in addition many a girl pretty, arrive in front of the Hôtel de Ville, walk into its forecourt, find it strikingly beautiful.

It seemed appropriate to compliment a waitress from the Jura, and I accepted my meeting a young man from the Aargau as a whim of fate. We walk through a gigantic department store and at an outdoor café sit cosmopolitanly in the fresh evening air.

The inhabitants of Geneva seem open to the world and friendly. I buy almonds, give them to boys, withdraw from their company, since each time I'm in a new environment I quickly become accustomed to it, then sat in the Petit Casino where a comedy was performed, and hunted up a bar where dancing was going on.

On my evening promenade I came to the little island in the River

---

*A 1922 German film, *Lucrezia Borgia*, directed by Richard Oswald, starring Conrad Veidt and Liane Haid. Walser walked from Bern to Geneva in the autumn of 1923.

Rhône, adorned by its monument to Rousseau, and took my hat off to the immobile one who evoked so much movement.

The city's location on the lake confers on it something gentle, calm. Splendid hotels line the quay. The bridges over which you stride exhilarate you. For a long time, I followed with my eyes a slender woman who reminded me of someone.

In the Schweizerhof, though it was late, I still found desirable accommodation for a reasonable price. The return journey was by train, which traversed the distance that took me two days to walk in four and a half hours.

1925

THE YARDSTICK

A GIRL lost her yardstick; I didn't pick it up for her, she'll have to find it again herself. She has a suitor who nimbly pursues and calls on her; she, however, finds his visits intrusive. His unkempt beard causes her concern; he does indeed wear it too long, and he's widowerish, and his widowerishness contributes to her aversion as well. If I were Fräulein Helgeli, I would accept him, but since I'm not, I'll confine myself to admonitions, namely: "Take him!" But what good is advice? She wants me but doesn't know I am otherwise engaged. Ten want me. What chance is there for one? If I were Fräulein Helgeli, who has a speech defect she should consider, I would attract the music teacher, who would be there on the spot, and I wouldn't look to me, who in turn have also lost my yardstick, which no one picks up for me either and I must find again for myself. The beard-bearer probably lost his sense of proportion, too, in daring to look upon Fräulein Helgeli, who refuses him admission, as she'd rather admit me, though she should know how easily I can do without stopovers, as befits a gentleman, since I'm already involved. "Take the beard!" I would like to shout at Fräulein Weigeli. "Don't you think you could also live nicely with beards?" She doesn't listen and thus pays the price. She spends her nights alone instead of in proper company and doesn't pay her measuring stick any heed.

I'm still young, my mouth is fastidious, my heart already taken, and her speech impediment alienates me as much from the one with good intentions as her lover's beard alienates her. She repudiates him because he's widowed, I repudiate her because it's proper to do so, I who can find admission elsewhere. Young things I gladly kiss, he too, she too, and everyone else as well. Am I the one who made the laws of nature? I would be proud of such a feat, of which I don't boast. Before long

Miss Bäldeli should accept the old man graciously; he yearns for her, I don't, hence I'm not the deciding factor. Rather than see her happiness in satisfying the harpist, she sees it in futile fancies. Odd that so many of us pursue a delusion. This knowledge weighs heavily on me but doesn't prevent my regretting that Fräulein Zeltli for her part pities the flautist, for which I deny all responsibility. There's something offensive about hoping. Hopeless love is the proudest. In vain Fräulein Geldli hopes to lure me with her money, in vain her admirer courts her, and when it's evening and the palace—where lives the one whose smile bewitches me—is fabulously illuminated, I strum away in vain on my mandolin. Modesty is an adornment that ornaments happiness, to which the yardstick pertains. Lucky for those from whose minds it doesn't slip away.

1926

FOUR CHARACTERS

THE DEVIL: In my opinion, that I am a poor man isn't often enough taken into account. My discontentednesses deserve commiseration. It's not unlikely that my homeland is Peru. One of the greatest poets who ever lived lavished a substantial amount of time on me, attempting to sketch my clearest and most comprehensive portrait, and in no sense did he fail. Goethe set forth irrefutably how gifted people in particular, for example university professors, urgently require the devil's assistance. Witty, erudite people often act rather ineptly vis-à-vis life and its exigencies, and if they still want to pluck the pleasures of existence, which we cannot hold against them, whether they like it or not they're compelled to rely on me and my incontestable scoundreldom, which in itself alone seems enticing to them. Yet what happens once I've been of service, have liaised?

ANGEL: Then you are despised.

DEVIL: And naturally you think I deserve it.

HYBRID BETWEEN ANGEL AND DEVIL: Don't argue; take my superb serenity as a model. I'm neither evil nor good, neither kind nor wicked, neither very valuable nor valueless. I'm half fish, half plant, constrain myself in every respect, am as far removed from utter vice as I am from full-fledged virtue. In professing a serpent's writhing cornucopia, I get along with everyone, if need be. Nor have I ever been seen as highly cheerful or very ill-tempered. I'm insouciant because I'm decent, that is, I'm never completely without worry.

DEVIL: I have to curse and rage and concern myself continually with sins of all degrees and classes. In time this becomes a bit monotonous. My villainies strike me as vapid. Within me there lives something that longs to become kind and useful. By now the wanton ones, whom I unremittingly have to deal with, are boring company. And then there's this: the devil's métier isn't modern.

ANGEL: Is that also true for my métier? If the devil disappears, must not the angel as well? This question could make me melancholy. Do, please, stay what you are.

DEVIL: Always these miserable seductions!

ANGEL: But then that would indeed be the end of my divine mission. Do bear that in mind a little. Have some regard for me. For quite some time you haven't been devilish. I sense that with keen regret.

DEVIL: Do you feel forsaken?

ANGEL: I suffer from a dearth of activity. Everywhere there is a lack of the fallen. Why did you stop asserting yourself? I'm so beautiful when the hopeless implore me for redemption and those ensnared for deliverance.

HYBRID. From the bottom and silence of being itself I have to laugh at you both. You're extreme and thus hilarious.

DEVIL: There's not much going on in hell anymore.

ANGEL: No one needs heaven now.

DEVIL: This is due to my influence.

GOD: I bend down over my thoughts. The youth is lying fatigued in the open countryside. Around him his energies smile. Genii glance about with big eyes. The world waits. I am the motionless motion. Ah, to be so unique!

1926

NOTEBOOK EXTRACT

THIS PROSE piece may resemble a joke.

There are, for me, circumstances, connections, of a curious sort. Perhaps there exist inferences, consequences no one is capable of perceiving.

I remember a little basket and a large, strange house. Near it a lake towered, as it were, blue. Of course, that sounds a bit comical, fanciful. We can heighten impressions into the bizarre. From a certain ethical, sculptural standpoint that's permitted. Lakes towering mountainously up, albeit like silk scarves lying as quiet as a mouse—it's all right to laugh at them, that causes no harm whatsoever. Every day, early in the morning, the aforementioned little basket was lowered by a woman for the postman to put the letters in. Something was wrong with the woman. Perhaps she suffered from migraines. In any case, she was a puzzle to me. In this house, I once spoke with a young aristocratic lass. I did that because at the time I was something like an assistant, and while I answered all sorts of questions from her I busily addressed envelopes. I was a kind of private correspondent. May I request that no offense be taken at that wonderful lake corresponding in its smoothness to a polished checkerboard that nevertheless apparently curved and reared up? I concede the comicality inherent in this oddity, and now I shall speak about the gist of the matter, namely, Napoleon III, who, as everyone knows, wore a dainty beard and was quite the elegant figure.

As has been proven, this great man lost an important, momentous war. Incidentally, he spent part of his youth as an aspiring rifleman in the small town of Thun with its splendid four-turreted castle forming the gateway to the Bernese Oberland. For a time in Thun, my insignificance drew breath as a savings-and-loan clerk, and in this same town Heinrich von Kleist composed his comedy *The Broken Jug*, which once spectacularly flopped in Weimar. At the same time, in the pretty country house still to be seen near Thun, the poet in question arduously exerting himself, alas in vain, with tragedy-writing, approached the creation of the *Robert Guiscard* material. Of this he left us an interesting fragment.

Napoleon III, it's told, one day poked disparagingly with his walking cane, which he was in the habit of taking with him wherever he went, at the surface of a Courbet painting that hung in some Parisian gallery or other. The picture didn't seem to impress him. Do I perhaps mean to imply that Napoleon III lost a war because he caned around in a work of art? By no means do I; rather, I content myself with referring you to the abovementioned, the part that relates to the strangeness in the realm of connections. There can be major artists and minor rulers. No one will think it necessary to doubt this possibility.

Napoleon III mainly stood out because he had a beautiful wife named Eugenia. She had the most fabulous wardrobe and revealed a demeanor whose magic no one who was afforded the chance to behold it could escape.

Moreover, it's strange that Count von Bismarck, the opponent of the one under discussion, read Heine with pleasure. After all, Bismarck was a conservative. What to make of such a preference in taste, such a predilection? This doesn't seem like a difficult question to me. With his gift for language, though principally, to be sure, with the abundance of his brilliant wit, Heine amused the Prussian count.

So, a fan of Heine's had good fortune, while an enemy of Courbet's met with misfortune.

It's well known how Emperor Wilhelm of Germany, who lost the World War, often railed at so-called *Rinnsteinkunst*, that is, gutter art. Under *Rinnsteinkunst* he also erroneously included Delacroix. Once, he uttered rather disparaging remarks about this eminent person in the realm of painting. On one occasion, accompanied by a friend, I visited the artist Max Liebermann, from whose mouth I heard what I have just expressed.

In this case things didn't go as well for the undervaluer of Delacroix's as he had wished.

Once, in Karlsbad, strolling along the promenade there, Goethe and Beethoven conversed vivaciously and extensively about this and that. In this world-famous spa, Edward of England once sat in the theater and watched the one and only Grete Wiesenthal dance. However, she danced, as it were, too unpretentiously for him, too ineffectively, too much like a joyful, happy woman, overemphasizing the heartfeltedness, the naturalness. Heartless, Edward left the auditorium while Wiesenthal was still dancing. But lo and behold, this inconsiderate person, well versed in the ways of the world, this person who found Grete Wiesenthal impossible, met with good fortune.

How to explain this?

Edward VII admired the art of ballet, of dancing on point. Natural dancing didn't correspond to his criteria. Vis-à-vis Grete Wiesenthal, he was, in a sense, right. In this case, he gave proof of what he had found occasion to demonstrate in other instances: his expertise. The artist in question seemed to have behaved in an insufficiently restrained manner for his taste.

Let me step away from this essay.

If I were a romantic person, perhaps I would shed a tear. This is only a notebook extract.

1927

THE YOUNG SERVANT

BUSY WITH carpet-beating, he wondered if his mistress was beauti-ful, and as he was cleaning the silverware he was conscious that he loved her with a dumbstruck, precious dispassion.

Little swallows whirred around on the roof, his affections dashing shimmeringly about him and flying round the woman, whose husband was inexpressibly elegant. Not to mention the tenderness of the daugh-ter, whom the young servant quite easily respected, considering adora-tion of the baby daughter inappropriate, since he was of the opinion that such little figures belonged to some future prospect.

Carelessly he brushed the husband's coat and dusted étagères where selected literature slumbered as soundly as Sleeping Beauty. The ques-tion whether he was capable of polishing the mistress's little boots had first been seriously discussed before consent was given.

During his boyhood he had played cowboys and Indians with his pals in the vicinity of the romantically situated village of his birth, and, still carrying his schoolbag on his back, he experienced an early love for a descendant of stage players, with her hair that seemed to laugh and effervesce like spring water, and from whose eyes faraway regions glistened back at him.

Now he found himself as if in the power, so to speak, of a woman who had never seemed to think it necessary to bark at him, since to her he appeared much too young and inexperienced for that.

It goes without saying that she was satisfied with him, because had she not been she would have perceived him as a bother, and then all she would have had to say to him was: "Leave us!"

Without intending it, the maidservants instructed him in the art of evincing a pleasant appearance. He found them amusing, and they him as well. In addition, the clean dishes in the kitchen alone made him cheerful.

The house wherein he served stood like a palatial office building in one of the most frequented streets of the city, which he always compared to the town where he had grown up long ago.

If I describe the young servant as having been happy practicing his profession and add the remark that perhaps this wasn't only because of the carpets he beat or due to the silver he cleaned or as a consequence of the arrival of those he adroitly announced, I do go a bit far, I know it.

Here, by the way, I was inspired by an illustration.

1928

A LACKEY

THIS TIME my assignment, which turns me into a kind of schoolboy, strikes me as something fresh as alpine air. Lucky for me I'm a schoolboy and not a lackey.

Since the beginning of time all spurious lackeys have felt themselves thoroughly *lackiert*, that is, swindled. With what precision I say this!

My lackey wasn't born a lackey. That is, throughout his life he couldn't make out if he had been chosen to banquet or serve at the manorial table. At times he lived in a most charmingly located house of a darling woman, who little by little instilled in him a talent for tenderness.

If I protest that he was no schoolboy, I accuse him all the more of having one day been told to go to the devil.

Someone said to him, "Get the hell out of here," and the lackey soul went on his way.

He was, in a sense, despotic. Shall I immediately prove this allegation? One evening, as he was accompanying a little lady, who was eight years old, to the theater, observing a well-measured distance, he fancied himself entitled to feeling, as far as human and civic pride were concerned, offended and oppressed.

One might say, thin as he was, that he was two and a half meters long or tall.

The ludicrous thing was that he was doing literary work alongside his lackeying. If a lackey possesses the impertinence to be belletristically busy, then he's a smug striver who can't reconcile himself with the requirements of his profession. Once, apropos of his being stupid enough to break to smithereens a precious cup in spite of all his intellect, he received a slap in the face, an occasion on which even his being called a rascal did not appear to meet with his consent.

He lacked the passion to be what he was. A pity his face had a nose that boasted no resemblance to a real lackey's nose.

He felt it necessary to take to the road and, from time to time during his journeys, to think back on his days as a lackey, which had afforded him the chance to learn to understand life.

With a series of anti-lackeyish writings, which he drew from his heart's longing for freedom, he made sure that others started to believe in him. Nonetheless, he begrudged mankind the influence he brought to bear upon it.

When asked in the rooms he entered about his background, he replied: "Once, I was a lackey."

Well, I never!

1928/29

A SORT OF NARRATIVE

I KNOW I'm a kind of artisan novelist. A writer of novellas I most definitely am not. If I'm in a good mood, that is, in high spirits, I cut, cobble, forge, plane, knock, hammer, or nail lines together whose contents are immediately comprehended. I could be called, if you like, a literary lathe operator. When writing, I'm wallpapering. That a few friendly people believe themselves entitled to call me a poet, I indulgently and politely concede. In my opinion my prose pieces are nothing other than parts of a long, plotless, realistic story. For me, the sketches I produce now and then are shortish or more extensive chapters of a novel. The novel I am constantly writing always remains the same one and could be described as a multifariously cut-up or ripped-apart book of the self.

An elderly, thus practically aged or, in fact, even somewhat, i.e. rather utterly old man, whose silvery glistening hair a kind, docile valet brushed or combed every morning, believed himself justified to think and at any time blithely declare that two persons who were his sons evinced two quite different aspects. Somebody or other is delivering me a certainly very uplifting, nifty motif here, which, for the time being, I don't wish to reveal. Who is it, who is offering me this charming subject matter to adapt?

I could imagine that I was in an old but nonetheless bright, sunny, cheerful room furnished with a stove from former times on whose tiles, from which it was constructed, I could see a story depicted, each scene affording me insight into an interesting course of events.

The first sonny is handsome, though at the same time, relatively speaking, unfortunately dissolute, while the second sprout, with a not-too-portly appearance, by which I mean to say not particularly favorable figure, distinguished himself by his sobriety. The first offspring wandered far and wide, while number two, nicely proper, helpful, and polite, stayed at home, where the lover of the first son has ample opportunity to think vividly, I mean longingly, of the one who betook himself up and away, in other words, the fervent and idealistic one who now, in all likelihood, roamed about poor and lost in uncertainty. What the characters are called shall not be blabbed.

The one endowed with every gift of note, now and then, perhaps, has nothing to bite or break, by which could be meant to eat. Possibly his suit has begun gradually to show signs of neglect, and whether he has the opportunity to get a shave regularly seems questionable to both himself and his stay-at-home girlfriend, who is of a sensitive nature. Nonetheless, she loves him all the more for such interesting dubiety. Now and then the old progenitor, or patriarch, draws the girl into the spell or circle or frame of a conversation in which it may occur to him to say: "My son yearns to come home, and while this in itself certainly splendid characteristic renders him a caring person from head to toe, he wanders through once rich and powerful, yet now half-ruined cities enchanting to every eye appreciative of art, because of the ruination, or he climbs over screes and inclines, and encounters marching past him citizens in dubious company colorfully woven together, who seem to carry along some sort of mission on their shoulders, and sees them enter this or that imposing or inconspicuous door. Where are you now, hope of my frailty?" And he wrings his hands, if you can accept that as credible, and the young miss knows nothing better to do than imitate him as regards his pitiful demeanor. It's evening; the other son, uninvited, takes the liberty of entering into the hushed, tall, quiet room. "Get out!" they both shout at him as if with one voice. "What?" he replies, taking a bold stance, and all three, as if astonished by themselves, stand remarkably immobile, utter nary a syllable, until the girl, to give her soul the peace that in every respect it needs, sits down at the piano and plays as exaltingly and splendidly as one could expect.

The house wherein all this takes place has been standing since olden times in a capacious garden with a diverse variety of plants and crisscrossed by numerous paths. On the next day an unknown man, his face carefully covered by a mask, announces himself to the landlord.

What was it he wanted? "Not much," he lets them know. So, he's asked to enter. He steps inside and tells them that the one the fair maiden has desired and longed for is no more. Labors, called hardships, of all sorts had been stronger than he and had overcome him. When the, incidentally no doubt excellent, old man heard this fairy tale, he collapsed. The servants felt compelled to come running, lifted him off the floor, and carried him to his bedroom, where they carefully laid him in bed until a doctor arrived. The girl fled into her boudoir, and the very solemn second son, this, it appears, immense rapscallion, danced for joy in the hall, displaying all kinds of agility.

What did he say, other than: "Now I'm the master," and doesn't the source, as it were, that nourishes me, peek or blink through the alpine meadow on which, so to speak, I graze my fill?

Meanwhile, Son Number One is experiencing different things: on a beautiful afternoon he rests in the posture of repose upon a hill adorned by idyllic nature, beneath the pergola of a few trees invigorating in orderly disorderliness this genial place, and, as he receives a visit, thinks back on the kindnesses of his boyhood, the loveliness of family life, everything endearing that once surrounded him. The one who has come to see him discloses that she still loves him. The one who hears this leaps up, immediately lets his intention to go to her—so that he would see her and she him—be known, and in fact a reunion occurs.

It will have been noted that Schiller's *Robbers*, which I've recently treated myself to again, has induced me to become serious and made me laugh, which is of a piece with poetry, so to speak.

A few posters I noticed yesterday at the train station spontaneously served me regarding the landscape decoration.

In quite a few rooms you'll find ovens worth seeing.

1928/29

FAIRY TALE (II)

I'M RELATING here a perhaps in part preposterous story.

For quite some time things had been going splendidly for me; what's more, one day I inherited an altogether only trifling sum, which enabled me to live free of worries. The days that lay before me resembled a bewitchingly beautiful, ornately furnished apartment.

What a prosaic comparison!

With the utmost leisureliness I evolved into something of a gallant who, among other things, amused himself by writing poetry in his spare time. I knew I was something of consequence, or I easily fancied myself such.

Pretty fantasies, as you know, make us happy.

Now I shall speak of the one whom I loved and toward whom I delighted in demonstrating my affection.

At one and the same time she was a little and a lot, and so was I. Now I was the universe, now only an atom in the universe.

May I hope to be allowed to think this philosophy? How splendid it was when I could sense my self-assurance, my elegance intimidating her. This elegance, however, might also only have been a figment. When I saw my love being timid, I found her enchanting.

Now comes something apparently quite fantastic.

To my amazement, suddenly I lost my previously snappy, bold, slender figure. Some unknown power transformed me into a ball; I became quite round and instead of walking I rolled and bowled along.

She saw me, and when she realized what I had become, she shrugged her shoulders and made fun of me, as well as seeming amazed or surprised by my appearance. Likewise, she was induced to feel indignant, which one will easily find oneself capable of understanding.

For my part I was pleased with the situation I found myself in, though I certainly didn't dare regard it as awesome.

At first my beauty didn't know how to regain her composure and hence gave me a kick, albeit only a small, delicate one, which stayed in my memory.

Years have passed since then. In the course of time I've assumed new forms.

1928/29

BOOK REVIEW

HOOEY was the name of a female bit player in the movies; it was more a waggish than a piquant, elegant name.

The story played out in Paris. The streets shimmered cosmopolitanly. I don't wish to take this too far. The present book review will boast only scant range. That's what we're dealing with here. The twinkling, whispering Eiffel Tower immersed its gigantic shape fairytale-like into the mirror of the Seine.

The author of the little booky confides to me that Hooey had operated the typewriter before she embarked on a career in the movies and got to know a movie chap, or man, who suggested without the least ado that she become his mistress.

Aggrieved, she said to him, "How do you come by this arrogance that induces me to be astonished before the eyes of an otherwise apparently quite passable person undeserving of being present at such a scene?"

She left, and the first movie man was as good as done for.

In the eveningness she made a, certainly at first, still-indecipherable, dark, but nonetheless gradually brightening acquaintance in the form of Movie Man Number Two, who appeared capable of appreciating Hooey's sensibility.

In delicacy, deference, etc., he resembled a hitherto-never-before-beheldness. He didn't say right away to the helpless, pretty girl: "I love you and invite you to dominate me." He waited, tapping her hand in the meantime and saying, "Oh, you artist," a remark that instilled her with trust in him.

Girls, especially the beautiful ones, aren't fond of being indelicately, incautiously reminded of the so-called purpose of their existence, which is sufficiently well known to themselves; their affections are most likely gained by someone adept at sidling around the all too obvious. Beauty is always, as it were, prudish, and needs to be felt, comprehended, tolerated.

Be that as it may, Hooey, on the basis of a thus favorable agreement she entered into with the second movie man, acquired a splendid apartment.

I read the little novel swiftly and at the same time tranquilly. The windows of my room stood open; from outside the voices of passersby seeped into my literary pursuits and abode which, for the sake of the present experiment, I wish to call a book review studio.

One day Hooey's heart began to declare itself, in that she conveyed the news to her benefactor, whom she felt entitled and obliged to regard as such, that she preferred to leave him and go back to typewriting.

Upon taking delivery of the declaration of her decision, the recipient of her letter containing the announcement said: "She loves me, and since luckily I love her as well, and probably the only reason why she would prefer not to love me would be that somehow she acquired the chance to take notice of my love, she seems to be a precious valuable and we both seem suited for conjoining."

In fact, she became his.

Somewhere in the morning breeze, or evening glaze, islands rose from the sea.

Elsewhere, someone seeking a devotional service might have been entering a cathedral.

High up in the mountains lay eternal snow.

Yet again fresh proof of my sedulity in the practice of literature seems to have come off as quite strange.

1928/29

VACATION (I)

THE WAVES splash in the bay. Surely I'm lying when I claim this, but we do say anything to get something going. In fact, the bay is in motionless repose. The repose could just as well be called silence; this stillness is beautiful, it has to be, I desire, want it. Am I now on vacation in the country, and is it in a sympathetically restored Gothic castle that I'm presently modestly residing? With a strange solemnity, a swan brings me news I can't comprehend, but nonetheless seems eloquently incomprehensible. The rooms or chambers of the castle have a wonderful grandeur. How eagerly and often people today employ the wordlet "wonderful." There is always some kind of tree, a picture, a girl, a movement, a remark, a region that's wonderful. Bathing is wonderful, riding as well. A few ask which is more wonderful: composing or not composing. The curtain at my narrow window, which has a windowish physiognomy, seems to be smiling; in a moment of introspection I wonder whether or not this smile is directed at me. There is something curious about the anima of an object, and on the whole being idle may be somewhat odd, somewhat good, and somewhat tiring. I can assure you that it's my tirednesses that are doing the writing here. For the most part it's they who look into life joyfully and vivaciously. At times a boat, in which someone sits playing music, glides past the house. To name the instrument seems superfluous to me. This assertion might be a frankness that could be agreeable as well as inappropriate. The omission of a name, of a designation, is not a lie and has an invigorating effect, because every denotation, so to speak, is old and wearies us. I don't know whether or not I might make myself believe that it was refined of me to write to a woman: "May you never weary." The food I prepare myself, which I by no means needed to stress here, because by so doing, a sketch that should be romantic is imposed upon. A library afforded me the opportunity to read a few books. While I read, it rained, as though it was meant to be thus, as though wet weather was befitting for escaping the things of the present. Reading, by the way, need not always be done only by those at a loss for something to do, because of an emptiness one feels obliged to fill. I paid close attention to a book that was snappily composed, as well as to another that was composed totally otherwise, a simultaneously sloppily and indifferently scribbled tome. Possibly my attention was too attentive. At times I feel inclined to see myself as too intense. Often, we lack sufficient courage to be frivolous. For example, perhaps walking is just as harmful as it is useful, since while doing so we can learn to adore solitude and gradually forfeit social skills. How nicely I managed to put this! I'm seldom a nice person, but I find I have reason to believe this is proper. Being well behaved can be celebrated by those who are.

1928/29

FRAGMENT

THIS CHILD was among the most diligent in school. Had Mary Stuart not been beautiful, she would never have experienced many experientialities. The one of whom we're speaking had the good fortune often to be allowed to stand on the riverbank and to be employed in an office, where he embezzled a box of matches. Others, in order to develop adroitness, trot off with the cash register without a trace. One evening, as he walked over a field, our lad saw a lamp burning in a room; quickly, he went home and thought long about the lighting apparatus. Then he married a widow, which would be exceptionally nice if it were true, but it was only an idea of his. Because he looked so in need of protection, sometimes he found friends. For a while he gave lessons in sweethearting. The sky had the deep, blushing-with-joy blue of a little frock fluttering around pretty legs, which without doubt constitutes a rather serious contemplation of nature. I pass over an English bed and travel to Naples where I've never been but where a man found a woman benevolent enough for him to hit her up for a loan. She told me this at dinner while peeling and slicing a pear for me. For a good while a not-disingenuous conversation was held about a worthy school of poetry consisting of people who always prefer to pacify themselves rather than write too much and thus perhaps bring themselves to ruin. Then he went into a soap factory, if only here on paper, which is absolutely unresisting: Schöneberger Ufer* is enchanting. Once, a luminary, that is, a highly influential gentleman, approached me while I was speaking with a beautiful woman; in this circumstance there resided something slightly insulting about that personage, precisely

*A street where Walser once resided in Berlin that runs along the Landwehr Canal.

the reason she talked to him through her nose. In contempt there sometimes lies something impotent: an effort that bears no fruit.

Then, late one night, he came to a villa and rang the bell with the circumspection bestowed upon him by his father and mother, whereupon the drawbridge rattled down and a giant appeared who invited the newcomer to follow him, telling him the female inhabitants were asleep. There are two varieties of youthfulness there, one natural, but also one acquired. A pig was there, in the company of highly refined people who took it out for a walk, but it only pouted. Once, there was a lavishly gifted, rosy-cheeked corpse, a pity it dressed so negligently. The new arrival, crossing over the drawbridge that afforded him admission to the family in whose bosom he would henceforth dwell, directed a word of recognition to the doorman, composed a sonnet, and walked up stairs without a carpet but colorfully covered with feathers and thread, to arrive at a door that one of the daughters opened to him, expecting him to love her, otherwise she would tell Mama, who then would whisper, "Wicked man!" Story rich in content, where are you taking me? Again, I've run out of stimulating tobacco. Accompanied by reproaches, retiring for the night after having only just arrived, he went up to his room and locked the door behind him. Early in the morning his gaze fell on a tablecloth embroidered with the words "Look up happy and gay at the break of day." Fully intent on breakfasting, he went into the dining room where three cats stared at him, the first of whom asked how he had slept, to which she added one does well to leave youthfulness to the young. Coffee was poured into waiting cups to the sound of bells ringing from the next village. A conversation ensued to which the Alps seemed to be listening from afar. Lofty listeners, aren't they? It was love that was being spoken of. The theme arrives as if of its own accord. Once, one of the daughters had been revered so devotedly by a waiter that he received for his betrothal gift the return of the same, wherein he could harbor his devotion with which she didn't know what to do. For her part, the second daughter had once proffered her devotion to an office clerk who returned the gift with a snub for her to neatly store her dreams in. While she made known her story, she fiddled around with her hair until it curled over her shoulder. The mother yawned and Siegmund thought it was meant for him. Then came days and nights filled with little domestic matters. The nights had the appearance of inexplicable birds spreading weariness with their wings. "Once, a young woman I had laughed at told me that I, too, might once again have to heave a sigh, and now I don't know which of you two I should love," said the one almost approaching the end of his breakfast, whereupon they giggled. Let's step away for a moment from the villa. A face is looking at us. Who is it?

In Wilmersdorf a maid told me she had been the mistress of her mistress. Around the great hall, court pages lay stabbed to death. The princess delighted in the beauty of the death rattle, although it might be permitted to question the beauty of this sentence. She stood at the vaulted window and, a silhouette enshrouded by evening light, looked over the quietly breathing, unsuspecting lake, upon which the bent saber of the moon gazed down with a silvery indifference. True beauty doesn't move. How much farther a peaceful handshake reaches into the joy of living than a kiss that is absorbed. It seems marvelous to me to gently pester an angel with my eyes. But gliding along on the wave of my novella, I now allow the little idiot to stroll into the night bending maternally over the earth, with one of the aforementioned countesses, who said, "Why isn't it possible for you to cherish me somewhat less but instead treat me more courteously? Is my intelligence the cause of that? Is it due to the fact that my behavior, my character, only engages your intellect?" With both herself and him having thus guessed right, he left the question unanswered. Then they spoke of the characters in Gotthelf's novels. Daily, the countess went to the office, which goes to show that daily she summoned the energy to face the truth. The narrator might be permitted to fabulate that there was once a country where a prince combed the hair of his servant girl. On a caustic note, I once ripped apart a two-hundred-page manuscript. For our Siegfriedli there came a time when the people wearing black armbands disconcerted him. By the way, my beloved found me boring because lovers bask in their love and thereby naturally do wrong. Let me think about the brave girl in America named Edith who dropped a handbag full of letters that someone took with him to have power over her. The scoundrel loved her, but she despised him. Having but little regard for him, she paid him no regard. He took advantage of this heedlessness. Edith in the hands of someone unprincipled: what a scandal! She trembled before him, and he rejoiced, with his little purse full of evidence, and trembled as well. The guiltless one quaked like the guilty. Then they chanced upon each other in the forest, and she drew her revolver. The book cover was indeed also quite exquisite. Hesitantly, he reached into his overcoat and, his face pale, pulled out what was desired. She has turned out a bit thin, strong nose, a noselet would suffice. With its feather plunging down in back, her hat makes an impression. Skirt short. Magnificent how he succumbs to her threat. Since then I can't shake free of this Edith. Recently I sat in a restaurant and stared out into the street in the hopes of seeing her pass. But it didn't occur to her to show herself, which I found proper. There are wishes we don't wish to see fulfilled because they are too dear to us. If they were fulfilled, they would be lost. The desire to see her means more to me than her appearance. Meanwhile Siegmund, who was supposed to be writing a good book, sat at the edge of the forest next to Lina on a bench painted green, then in the late evening in a pub where a woman, telling him that she had once been young and pretty, acting on a sudden impulse of pity, smoothed down his disheveled hair. He had looked at her worriedly, the reason being the book, since he constantly thought about what was still unwritten. It was May. Betweentimes I often think about the Berlin trams, especially charming in the evenings. How joyful the sound of the compartment doors closing. Siegmund seems to like cleaning windows and gladly helps to transport furniture. Liqueur he disdains, but instead caresses little ladies' shoes. Now and then he takes rambles into the heights of the Emmental for recreation. The above-mentioned Lina, as a delicate breeze breathed through the shrubbery, told him she came from Nineveh. Our dolt should have long since dawdled along to Büderich, but Love with a capital L held him back, about which, bit by bit, I'll now speak with unprecedented ease.

I fear greatly for my hero. No hair do I leave unharmed on the one sauntering across fields, who perceived nothing more important on his ramble than a peasant woman swerving off to where, from time to time, we all discreetly swerve. It was night, and with the good book in his head—thus intent on generating literature—he paced slowly back and forth in front of a facade, drawing the attention of cabmen to his

Renaissance behavior. Everything around him appeared palatial. Children singing songs led a tiger on a pink ribbon, one of whom sat on the striped body, grinning about his sitting on God's creature. The night was bright in its not-being-able-to-get-darker and in its inability to be bright dark. Music effervesced from architectural edifices, now flowing into an obelisk, now bending flowerlike, now appearing in its sacred risings apparently intent on touching the stars that, like half-blind little eyes, blinked down on the scene where a door opened and Helen stepped forth, whom he addressed as follows: "Now can I have a word with you? You've had no time for the one who has thought all along about nothing but you and on every path only conversed with and in fever dreams fantasized about you, most tedious and divine one." "You speak both beautifully and unbeautifully. Feel free to express what you want to say, my friend," she said unperturbed. He continued: "I climbed through a concatenation of encouraging constellations, apparently high into life, in order, apparently, to fall. One is what one presents. You think of me as someone quite honest and insignificant, well disposed and piffling. I hear you attended the masked ball; for my part I, too, have already indulged in many pleasures I might have scorned. I gave you four hundred thousand francs." "Don't talk nonsense." "Sorry if I stumbled; I'd gladly be rich for your sake. How fervently you glowed once in a garden high above because I showed you a side of myself you hadn't counted on. At that time, I was rebelling against your beauty. Another time I simultaneously pleased and displeased you. I understand no one as well as you, but whether I can make you happy is unclear. In a Valais cloister, nuns looked fine on the stairs. I'm a friend of traditional customs." "Does that have something to do with what you want to tell me? Hurry up. The moment when I'll have to break off this conversation isn't far." She looked at him with a level sternness, without moving a muscle on her face suffused with charm, while he continued: "I know women who attempt to think little of me because of the influence you have on me." "Go to them," she replied and laid her hand on the door handle. "Where we stay, there we are deemed small. Only where we are missed can we be of much significance. But isn't happiness greater than greatness?" "Are those your friends roaming about there?" he was asked. "Acquaintances," he responded.

"By the way, I have to tell you that I owe the general public a book. For a frightfully long time I've been keeping them waiting. One shrugs one's shoulders concerning me. Perhaps you, too, wish I would conjure up perennial classics. I wandered around and found—you." Here he had to smile. Helen took offense at this.

Arriving at her apartment, she rang for the servants, who didn't come because none existed . . .

1929

WALK IN THE PARK

I HARDLY know how I should begin a story that perhaps plays out plotlessly. Once upon a time there was a girl who walked in a park that looked so beautiful she thought she could eat it with her soul. Something that we love effortlessly, such as a tree, a path, or a pond, however expansive it may be in reality, strikes us as small, graspable by the hand, as if we could pet it. To his lady, a polite lover seems something like a puppy or boy. The girl drew the park to her heart like a delicate beloved emanating from ideal lands and times, or she transformed the water, on which a swan swam, into a ring or a lovely, attractive bracelet, or she entered a little summer or garden house, like a bee with fine little wings and little legs slips and flies into an apiary. When one loves, one is small, and with what one loves it's exactly the same. If we perceive the beautiful as large, we're more likely to want to flee from it than be near it. How alluring heaven becomes if we imagine it inhabited by angels. When we think of it as boundless, we stand there bewildered. What roughly sketched babbling I've embarked upon here! A brook rushed babblingly, burblingly through a meadow that no one it seemed was of a mind to mow. The girl found firs standing scattered about giving voice to loneliness. As she regarded the fir branches dangling down like hair, she thought of old German copperplate engravings or etchings. When she stood at the edge of the pond, a swan swam toward her like a soft, cold flame, and she embraced the finely plumed beauty and kissed it with deliberate ease, while smiling superciliously about her friendliness. In knowledge she was not rich. To her Madame Mama she could never put a question, since the lady did not like to speak. Thus, the child was perhaps a bit neglected. Was her mother ill, was her illness something rich, vast, interesting, at which, usually sitting silently in her room, she stared in wonder? In a sweet, tiny cubbyhole, while the day was gazing with golden eyes through the window, the girl was reading amusing and at the same time thought-provoking little pieces by Molière, one of them entitled "La Princesse d'Elide," over whose quiet charm she prettily dreamed. Sometimes high society entered the park, caring, oddly enough, not much about either the mother or the little daughter. How loud then and life-affirming was the laughter! The legions, the multitude of spoken words! How erudite, clever all of them looked together! In a wing of the house opening out into, so to speak, seclusion, a boyish-looking poet, liberally and light-heartedly dressed in slippers and loose gown, poeticized at a dainty table and—over his thoughts, which he passed by as in a preciously decorated skiff or boat, and over his carefully recorded feelings that he might have extracted from the peculiarity of his being—wept as clear as crystal, finding the tears blissful without being saddened. From time to time the girl watched the strange person sympathetically.

1929

RECENTLY I READ...

JUST NOW I was speaking with someone, who doesn't need to be named, about Scheffel's *Ekkehard*, a book that once presumably caused quite a stir. A few years ago, by the way, comfortably ensconced as a houseguest, I began to read a novel by Raabe, who in his fashion brought forth delectable creations. Once you begin to read, it seems you're not able to come out of it. Here one is afforded the opportunity to occupy oneself with *The Black Tulip* by Dumas, which perhaps seems a bit too mannered, but nonetheless can be characterized as a captivating volume. On the other hand, Edgar Allan Poe's novellas possess that thrill that can carry you away and at the same time be intellectually spellbinding. It seems as though, regarding the American who lived only briefly, albeit devotedly, we are mainly dealing with a, as one surely might say, first-rate wordsmith, which doesn't come close to exhausting the praise this poet of the strange deserves. Among other modest books, albeit not unworthy of being read, there came into my hands a volume of the posthumous literary work of J. V. Widmann, who for a time was the literary editor of the Bernese journal *Bund* and as such achieved an excellence still recalled by many who could feel its effect.*
At the moment it is to a feuilleton novel entitled *Le Baron mystérieux* that I am devoting my attention, gladly surrounding myself every day with something gripping and yet nothing more than entertaining to me.

I wish to call Hauff's *Lichtenstein* a wonderful historical novel narrated by a youth for youths, by someone with a gift for illusions bestowed

*Walser's first publication, a selection of poems, appeared in 1898 in *Sonntagsblatt des Bunds*, edited by J. V. Widmann (1842–1911), who championed Walser's writing.

to others who possess the same, in which there is talk of a loyal person who finds himself most pleasingly rewarded for his pertinacity. A noble outcast temporarily holes up in a cave and, with his strength of character, attended by his handsome and agreeable appearance, is in the position, due to various contingencies smiling favorably upon him, to woo a young woman.

To return to Scheffel and his novel's character, whom I found occasion to mention at the beginning, there were a few pages I noted that interested me, whereby I engraved in my memory that a comfortable writing style, I mean an informal conversational tone, could be received as something quite serious. A book that, because it's neither contemporary nor fashionable, is read impartially, that is, calmly, perhaps can make you a little drowsy, but on the other hand also happy. Perhaps the essential point of reading is to gently isolate and pleasantly distract us from complexity, to erect something in the soul opposed by our too-lopsided participation in daily affairs. In Scheffel's novel one noteworthy passage revolves around a servant cheating his master, who places infinite trust in him, while giving his bread-giver, or prospective job-provider, to understand that he has his best interests at heart, though in reality this is by no means the case. Because he's thought of as a good person he has no desire to be good, while quite a few who are considered bad have not proven bad enough to justify the fame of being a villain.

Older ones, I mean books, that have been appreciatively read by generations that belong to the past, precisely for this reason alone exude something homey, which we gladly let ourselves be captivated by. The cloister in St. Gallen stands out architectonically on the shore of Lake Constance, which isn't to be taken as exactly geographically precise. Out of the surface of the lake arise the figures of Huns swinging swords over their heads.

Reading such things, we find ourselves being boys again, having parents, still attending school, flirting with the notion that we have pals. Shouldn't such temporary delusions be considered of value?

1930

THE FOUR SEASONS

IN SUMMER, so thought a young girl who was writing down her ideas on a sheet of paper furnished with dainty margins, flourish melons and cucumbers that one devours with delight. From elegantly shaped foliage, peaches and apricots peek out and smile like little easily adored eyes and cheeks worthy of being kissed. People walk around with the understandable wish that the weather remain constantly beautiful and the paths appear clean and dry. Under the murmuring shadows of the trees one can drink, chat, relax, and eat. By taking worthwhile excursions that perhaps aren't expensive, one has numerous human encounters and can inspect castles and churches from without and within while being looked at by woven and carved figures, of which it can be said that they are strange. In summer, mowing and harvesting take place. In the morning air, grain sways and waves back and forth melodically, the grass shakes and bends, and in the evening, with its elongated dimensions, striking us, as it were, as something slender, a woman with a slow, soft stride betakes herself into the chapel to pray in the cool, hushed building. The garden offers vegetables; on the water float gondolas decorated with little flags; country roads come alive with pedestrians and vehicles. Countless civil servants and businessmen, together with their families, enjoy the holidays in no way begrudged by others, until time commands them to return to their duties.

Quietly the apples and pears ripen; nuts begin to fall to the ground, which children carefully pick up and put in their pockets. Autumn is brief and forms a bridge as pretty as a picture, thus worthy of being seen, that leads from summer to winter. The diminishing of the length of the day is interesting, as well as the increasing or swelling of the night. Enchanting is autumn's brown hair, as if it were a Gypsy's, if I may allow myself a somewhat shabby, artless, naive, self-evident comparison that can't be spared the accusation of obviousness.

I have long wanted to write about the seasons. I seem now to have arrived at the third, a cold one, but behind the hard face hides a joyous, happy face, of which I will speak as soon as the moment has come. Wintertime distinguishes itself by its snowflakes and icicles, and by the fact that it's necessary to wear sweaters, overcoats, caps, and so on, and often to enjoy ourselves indoors in heated rooms. Forests, cities, mountains, and plains are as if sprinkled with flour or sugar, sleighs fly over the fields, little bells ring, and breath turns into something that visibly steams from humans and animals. Residents read books or honor the theater with their presence. Entertaining lectures are held. For months the trees are bare, no mosquito or fly can be seen, until gradually spring makes itself felt, with its florets and budding leaflings and the tantalizing whisperings from its mouth inviting us to stroll through the lovely green meadow, to offer a greeting to the warmth upon its return and gaze up at the sky where little clouds flutteringly promenade.

Once, I heard an oratorio in a village chapel that I believe had the same title as my modest little work, which I trustingly recommend to the public that, I tell myself, is a composite multiplicity, which delights me.

1931

STROLL (II)

THE FOREST was resplendent and laughed in its chromatic finery like a bride in Hungary respiring in her bedchamber in expectation of the bridegroom's arrival.

On supple paws in a park formed out of the wilderness, prowling tigers of India couldn't have displayed a more decorative, more tapestry-like speckledness than the branches with their distinctly colored foliage.

Resembling temples towering high, alpine peaks gazed chastely—recalling for me the sagas and snow country of Greenland—into the greenish coziness, through which I gave my legs permission to stride gently and vigorously at one and the same time.

Now and then I stood motionless, staring into my heart as into an America Columbus had yet to discover.

I came from afar, and in fact I seemed to have firmly in mind to go just as far, as if my blue or brown eyes envisioned my setting foot onto the shores of Australia.

For the time being, with the aid of my imagination, I was content to scurry through the Kazakh Steppe and climb the mountains of Argentina, which touch the edge of the sky with their jaggedness.

With birds of paradise my mind forged a friendship just as strange as it was confidence-inspiring.

Allowing myself the accomplishment of a respectful bow to the divinity of nature, I almost began to fancy myself a Japanese in the glow of the religions of the East, together with their figurations, when a hunter, wearing a feather-adorned hat on his head of Germanic shape, came cheerfully marching along, making me think of a coolly and thoroughly deliberative Germany whose manner of living might be labeled domestic.

Restlessly pursuing my many destinations, after a short while, on a hill Titianesquely enfragranced, a mandolin jingled in my attentive ear, transporting me in thought to Italy.

On the other hand, I carried a realistic Norwegian novel, hardcover or paperback, ready at hand in my pocket, so that now and then it might amuse and edify me.

The wonderful vast expanses of Russia, thin as greyhounds, floated toward me in the form of a plain adorned with birch trees scattered about, reanimating my spirit with persistence and a frisky endurance.

Whatever we need unfolds on its own; what's unnecessary stays undeveloped. My fatigue, like fields lying fallow, I had productively ploughed by means of my indefatigability, which to me resembled an attractive, industrious Negress, until, little by little, my walking brought me before a house that, because a girl resembling a Spaniard stood in the doorway, seemed to be an inn, so I went into the same.

Inside, as a reward for enduring the stresses and strains of walking and overcoming intellectual difficulties, I refreshed myself with a glass of wine.

1931/32

THE CASTLE

I READ a book. This was about eight days ago. I read it slowly. The carefulness with which I did it made me marvel at myself. I won't name the author, thus giving the readers of my article the opportunity to guess who it might be. Somehow and somewhere, he lived and wrote. That's enough. He may have had a wife in whom he inspired the pleasures of disappointment and the inconveniences of satisfaction. Life is difficult, art serene, a famous psychologist said at some point. But let's continue. The book's sorrows cheered me up. Its hero was a melancholic, a mechanic in being disconcerted everywhere and unceasingly by thoughts. He loved and was loved in return. Is that right? Strange question! He took life as tragic. Possessing excellent manners, he was grieved by the snow, with which he didn't know what else to do but find it beautiful and useless. Lenbach's *Good-for-Nothing* was his favorite painting.* There are images that everybody takes into their hearts with a smile, where they abide forever. In the spring he let the lovely singing of songbirds mock him. With a gaping wound in his soul he entered the meadow, on which he walked around until the evening recommended he seek the comforts of his castle chambers, where solitude pressed a kiss on his mouth. The noble ones walk about alone in life. On the other hand, moments of solitude embody a not to be underestimated wealth of possibilities to be free of pressure. Now I shall take half an hour or more to reflect before continuing to write. I

---

*The painting by the German artist Franz von Lenbach (1836–1904) that Walser has in mind is *Hirtenknabe* (*Shepherd Boy*, 1860), whose eponymous figure in repose on a hill recalls the narrator of Eichendorff's novella *Memoirs of a Good-for-Nothing* (1826).

do this for myself alone. At night the castle of the unlucky lover glistened like jewelry. His beloved seemed to be a woman who caused a thousand bothers. Housewives, while fraught with difficulties, often lack even an iota of humor. So it was with our character, who relished her solemnities. Woe is him whom she loved above all else as though he were indispensable. Often, she threw her arms around him and wept. Some men are predestined to be simultaneously favored and faulted by women. The enigmatic man seemed to be one of those. Manfully fighting his inclination to flee, he suffered unspeakably. "You'll never get away from me, you understand that?" Thusly or similarly did her innate childishness exert its influence on him. He compared the castle to a dream, the forest nearby to beautiful imagination. The book seemed to be written in an exceedingly fine prose. By my absorbing it, it changed into something, as it were, comfy. The female figure made a not entirely sumptuous impression, like women who constantly think about one and the same thing, who don't read because deep inside they already know everything worth knowing, who don't go out because they wish to remain quiet and not in the least question life. She knew he believed it was his duty to look after her. Yet she couldn't care less. She was indolent. Her lassitude drew him in. More and more he began to resemble her.

He and she and the castle were like a remnant.

I assume you're convinced I was reading a precious book.

1931/32

HATS

WE CALL a headpiece that's an ornament and at the same time useful a hat. Whoever thinks about hats first distinguishes straw hats from felt ones.

People who want to express that they are polite and considerate lift their hats civilly before the object to which they wish to pay their respects.

What is it that the word *Hut*, that is, hat, calls to mind? Caution. With the expression "*Hüte dich!*" or "Watch out!" one wants to warn oneself or someone else to keep within certain limits.

We may say or do many things but not everything. He who goes far takes care that he doesn't overwork himself or give occasion to cause offense.

The idea of *hüten*, that is, to guard or tend to, for example a flock or a sick person, seems related to the theme I'm dealing with. Otherwise we wouldn't speak of *Obhut*, that is, of guardianship. Moreover, a hut or house with a roof bears a resemblance to a hat.

In the past, to be cautious we wore hoods or masks that completely covered the face. We called this measure "masquerading." The knights of the Middle Ages wore helmets equipped with visors that could be opened and closed.

Instead of hats, women sometimes wore only a scarf they could wrap around their heads, conferring to themselves an appearance of prudence.

In such attire, old grannies told children fairy tales about wantonness, cunning, fear, and incessant activity.

Arabs wore head covering suitable for the region in which they lived. Indians of the Americas adorned their heads with feathers. The Basque wears a cap congruous with the Pyrenees.

Ladies of the Gothic period deposited extremely tall, pointed, sugarloaf hats on their hair. In the rococo and Empire periods the bonnet was the fashion.

Caps, if need be or circumstance requires, may be rolled up. This can't be done with bowler hats. From a hat that is becoming, one acquires a certain esteem.

Artists' hats are distinguished by a soft, undulating panache and a supple liberality.

How much finesse and attention over the course of time has been concentrated on the production of women's hats! Years ago, in a drawing room, I saw a portrait by Manet of a woman with a delightful headdress.

A young, beautiful woman would have been well disposed toward a nice young man if he hadn't been inclined to stroll along in a hat that displeased her.

A hat should tastefully conform to age as well as profession, but it's not recommended that you spend too long pondering this.

1932

SUNDAY OUTING

THERE'S something auspicious about an early-morning train ride. You sit comfortably among all sorts of well-mannered people who find you likable because they don't know you better. How it whizzes joyfully through the air! Little carefree clouds flutter behind the train. Water and country emerge into view. Objects draw nearer and recede. In quickness lies something exhilarating. One alights near a little town. This Sunday is warm; a woman unconventionally clad crosses the street. I climb sightseeingly up a medieval tower and find the view there resplendent. In my pocket lies a little dime novel I bought in a train station. After an hour it's refreshing to rest in a small birch forest. I have brought along provisions that now I consume. I stumble upon an inn on a hill where a wedding party, hair carefully coiffed and in part femininely bedecked with flowers and delicately veiled, is sitting at rustic-looking tables. Flies buzz about the summery room. There isn't much chatter, only here and there a little bit of a smile. The faces have red freckles and are full of character, and then I'm off again, up and down, past fields, farmland, flowers in bloom, and the sound that accompanies the blueness. How kind and beautiful the world is when you take a walk! In a ravine a brook glistens. The goal of my outing is a Renaissance castle that now, with its ornaments and turrets, begins to rise before my eyes in its full shape and stupendousness. I walk over an expressive bridge and enter the castle's extensive courtyard where I see a lady standing in a corridor. She stands motionless, and strangely wax-figureishly gazes toward me through the glass without paying me any notice. Meanwhile, a finely dressed girl has walked gracefully and with fitting pride across the courtyard, her agile legs joggling her frock, and an old attendant, whose appearance is quite respectable, turns up in an enchantingly and elaborately ornamented doorway. For a while I stand still, amazed, in front of all the grand architecture, then leisurely visit the park that's not closed to the Sunday public but instead calmly acquiesces to visitors contemplating it and enjoying walking back and forth along its numerous lovely paths. A pavilion with elegant columns and a picturesque roof adorns a hill. I almost imagine myself transported to the unreal, as it is with boys in the prime of youth who live in countries and regions that exist nowhere but in interesting books. Tall deciduous trees tower into the glorious airy heights. Gradually, evening begins to fall; songbirds sing soulfully, and a swan swims gently about on a round, lakelike body of water. How lush the meadows are, how beautiful this estate looks!

Soon the train takes me back whence I set off.

1932/33

THE CANAL

THROUGH a pleasantly situated landscape runs an artificially widened river whose width measures approximately twenty meters. It had been necessary to construct the canal at a time when the river's banks were often breached. Today, in the region I gladly speak of, no more devastations by flood occur, a circumstance about which the population in question can be delighted. To commemorate after his demise the creator of this significant beneficial correction, in the little village thought suitable for this purpose, that's to say on the spot where he grew up and acquired his knowledge in school, a memorial stone bearing his likeness was set up or approvingly and appreciatively erected. The aforementioned village belongs to the vicinity, it being in the center of the region under discussion. As regards the water of the canal, it flows or rushes less swift as an arrow than simply with a restrained, that is, moderate briskness to its destination, and in cleanliness and clarity doesn't leave much to be desired. I don't know with any certainty if it's at all of interest that I allow myself to bring up the fact that here and there nut trees grow along the canal's banks well suited for strolling. To the left and right of the muggy waterway, ranged over by mosquitoes and birds, runs a narrow little road. On either side lie meadows and fields that, as we say, stretch far and wide. Here one can walk and think undisturbed and promenade about for entire mornings and afternoons, as if one were the beneficiary of a solid pension, which as a kind of harmless insinuation may be apropos. Fruit trees adorn the plain, and for a distance of two hours the canal is paralleled by a mountain range whose rocky slopes glimmer delicately, as if they were wallpaper or trimming. Evenings on the femininely gentle and genially flowing water are, as is easily imagined, beautiful, and then, too, one or the other bridge leads over the mirrorlike slender spectacle of nature, if I might so call it, which I cherish like an enchanting apparition that now and then has made me happy.

1933

CHILDHOOD

HE WHO had begun to age thought more often now about his childhood. He found, for instance, the opportunity to understand that in many respects he had misjudged himself. New, I mean subtler, opinions and positions than had hitherto prevailed began to take precedent. Among other things, in spite of the accompanying shortcomings from which he would free himself only with assiduity, he thought he might hope to become a more sensitive person. Meanwhile, with genuine pleasure, he gave himself up to memories, which presented him with the stone staircase he used to climb up and down as a boy. The house in question held an air of distinction, its rooms had bright windows. In his early youth he liked to sit for a while in an office chair that swiveled and instilled him with confidence of a special kind infused with respect. A small staircase led down from the office into the store or shop that colorfully glistened with all sorts of luxury items. He could consider himself the descendant of tradesmen and admitted that there was hardly any other phenomenon he took keener interest in than the shed where many empty packing cases or freight boxes, stacked one atop the other, were stored. Abutting the little building was a tiny courtyard, in its turn bordered by a small alley. He often passed by a ceramic shop that produced pots, along with a carpenter's workshop across from it, also a small garden where thick bushes grew and now and then a little girl appeared. The fact that for many years he had devoted to his mother no or only fleeting thought was explained by his continual preoccupation with his profession, coupled with its concerns and hard work, the affairs of which led him now to this region, now that, which at least in part let him forget the one of his childhood. Into the street on which stood his parents' house flowed another street he strode down to get to school, a broad, pretty avenue that ran straight as a line, losing itself in the distant plain. The schoolhouse consisted of a long, two-story, monasterial, solid-looking building into which the scholarly flock entered through a huge gate in order to be educated by class and subject. What a strangely solemn impression he received from that instruction, which seemed equally liberating and subjugating, and wouldn't have been conceivable if it had not refreshed the heart just as much as it made it tremble. One was afraid and at the same time felt completely safe. In the schoolyard, where a row of low-hanging chestnut trees stood broad and umbrageous, the students organized games of chivalry where one made oneself available to the other as his horse, upon whom he boldly rode into battle to either hold his own or fall to the ground. What he ate during his boyhood seems to have escaped his memory, a circumstance that tends to prove that boys predominantly let themselves be led and influenced by spiritual matters. He might have been seven or eight when he encountered the sweet event that consisted of his noticing for the first time the twittering of the joyful inhabitants of the air. He learned to write and calculate, and acquired, with a kind of delight, knowledge in the areas of linguistics, geography, religion, and history. Among other acquaintanceships bestowed upon him as he was growing up, he familiarized himself with the charm and curiosity of the seasons. Feeling the warmth of summer and the cold of winter arose of its own accord. He learned both to favor and harbor antipathy toward others, moved in part in the circle of his friends, in part kept himself separate, as circumstance and chance allowed. Touching and giving rise to many an uplifting thought that set the mind astir for him and his youthful understanding was the holy figure of the Son of God. He professed Jesus to be his favorite, not so much consciously but lovingly and compassionately, without saying a word. It was splendid to display and show off to his mother what he had learned about heroic lore. Perhaps while retelling these tales, comfortably leaning on what had been committed to memory, he let himself be cheaply and undeservedly admired. Every now and then, by the way, he was caught out, for instance in front of the kitchen cupboard with his hand in the cookie jar. Once in a while, during his annual visit to one of his aunts, he received a suitable present. Between him and one of his classmates, quarrels alternated with reconciliations. It was natural for him to compare his mother to the mother of his friend. His mother suffered more than other women. Her longing for something she did not possess was passed on to him. He wished the restless one were at rest.

Little by little, he learned of the contents of the classics; he gazed into a wonderful world.

1933

BIOGRAPHICAL NOTE

BORN ON April 15, 1878, in Biel, Switzerland, Robert Walser left school at age fourteen to apprentice as a bank clerk. The pattern of his life was one of short-term jobs, mostly of a clerical nature, and short-term stays in furnished rooms. His poems and short prose began to appear in literary journals and in the feuilleton sections of newspapers in 1898 and 1899; his first book, *Fritz Kocher's Essays*, came out in 1904. Fourteen other books followed, including the novels *The Tanners* (1907), *The Assistant* (1908), and *Jakob von Gunten* (1909).

Walser's primary cities as a writer were Zurich (1896–1905), Berlin (1905–13), Biel (1913–21), and Bern (1921–33), though as a young man he also worked in Basel, Stuttgart, Thun, Solothurn, Wädenswil, Winterthur, and, after time spent at a school for servants in Berlin, six months as an assistant butler in Castle Dambrau in Upper Silesia. On Berlin Walser pinned his hopes as a professional writer. At times living with his brother Karl, already a successful painter, book illustrator, and stage designer for Max Reinhardt, Walser made inroads of a sort with editors, publishers, and the artists and clientele associated with the Berliner Sezession art gallery. But despite publishing three novels with Bruno Cassirer, as well as a book of poems, and contracting in 1912 with Kurt Wolff for two books of short prose, Walser's Berlin venture became a debacle of poverty and isolation. "I destroyed much that I had created with great effort. The more earnestly I longed and strived to put myself on a firm footing, the more clearly I saw myself teetering on the brink" ("A Homecoming in the Snow," *Berlin Stories*, trans. Susan Bernofsky, New York Review Books, 2006). In March 1913, he retreated to Biel.

When not stationed in various parts of Switzerland on military duty during World War I, Walser resided for seven years in an attic room of the hotel Blaues Kreuz. One might consider his several land-scape miniatures of 1914 and 1915, with their enchanted engagements with nature, as precise responses to the destruction raging in Europe. In a letter to Hermann Hesse on November 15, 1917, Walser addressed the role of the artist in time of war:

> You tell me you have wartime duties to perform.... For my part, I can assert, loud and clear, that my rifle stands, so to speak, ready for use, spick and span in the closet. I spent last summer in the Tessin [on military service]. The red wine was pretty good, we drank it like milk, a liter or liter and a half a day. Yes indeed, everyone is performing wartime duties now.
>
> Your remark that writers could do something does not seem unusual to me at all. The thought does come to mind, of its own accord. It may be wrong to sit, as I do, for example, in an expensive overcoat, inside an old Venetian palace, allowing oneself to be waited upon by seven hundred nimble servants.
>
> Word is going around that Robert Walser is leading the noble life of a dreamer, idler, and petit bourgeois, instead of "fighting." The politicians are dissatisfied with me. But what do people really want? And what great or good aims can be achieved by articles in newspapers and magazines? When the world is out of joint, the efforts of twenty thousand Hamlets are no use at all, or precious little. Every day I read a little French, because it is such a pretty language. Does that make me a rascal? And then I can't help walking around every day, a bit, in the winter countryside. Does that prove I'm indifferent to a great deal of suffering? I believe that you understand better than anyone why I like to live a quiet and thoughtful life. With friendly greetings from the marble palace I'm inhabiting, yours, Robert Walser.
>
> (trans. Christopher Middleton, in "Prose Pieces and Letters,"
> *Review of Contemporary Fiction: Robert Walser*, Spring 1992)

Although he published seven collections of prose and one of short plays while in Biel, in 1917 he wrote to one of his publishers that he had "done everything humanly possible by way of economizing. Good luck to anyone who wants to do the same." In addition to dining in soup kitchens, he did not heat his room in winter. With this in mind, a comic tour de force like "The Sausage" from 1917 takes on a grimmer aspect.

Between 1919 and 1933 he published only one book, *Die Rose: Skizzen* (The Rose: Sketches, Rowohlt Verlag, 1925). To Rascher Verlag, in 1919, he sent one of his typically brash cover letters:

> Today I am sending you my finished novel with the title
>
> TOBOLD
>
> 129 manuscript pages, separated into 35 chapters, each presenting a strong, precise picture. The work satisfies me. Perhaps it will please you as well. The novel sets itself apart from my earlier novels by its brevity. I request that you not let the manuscript get into *anybody else's* hands and to tell me *as soon as possible* whether you wish to publish it.
>
> Conditions have already been communicated to you. The book would have to appear *within this year*, perhaps in the fall. Please indicate receipt *immediately* and *at the same time* return "Kammermusik" [Chamber Music, a collection], as I want to do more work on it.

Of this lost novel we know that it concerned his years in Zurich. The completion of it produced this sprightly opening to Walser's "Snowdrops" (1919): "I've just been writing a letter in which I announced that I had finished a novel with or without pain and distress, that the considerable manuscript was lying in my drawer ready to go, with the title already in position and packing paper at hand, for the work to be wrapped and sent in. Furthermore, I have purchased a new hat which for the present I shall wear only on Sundays, or when a visitor comes to me" (*Selected Stories*, trans. Tom Whalen and Trudi Anderegg, Farrar, Straus and Giroux, 1982).

To the same publisher, in the same year, he submitted a collection entitled *Mäuschen* (Little Mouse):

> Please allow me to send you the enclosed manuscript for your consideration. Could you, if you like it, publish it soon, in time

for Christmas? I would like to ask you to reply as soon as possible and remain respectfully yours,

Robert Walser

P.S. It would make just a tiny booklet. The title indicates as much. In small format it would probably take up two printer's sheets.

In 1921, in search of new motifs, Walser accepted a position as assistant librarian at the state archives in Bern, where he lasted for only four months before making an "impertinent remark" to his superior. The following year he submitted another novel, *Theodor*, to both Rascher and Rowohlt, based on his time in Berlin as a secretary to Paul Cassirer, the director of the Berliner Sezession gallery. Though this manuscript also vanished, a twenty-five-page fragment appeared in a literary journal and begins:

The cigarettes come from Reinhold, this genius of a businessman. He motioned to the box with a sideward glance. Instead of only one I grabbed two handfuls, which impressed him, even though from time to time he might complain about me. Let him. The main thing is that he believes he can use me.

Will I disappoint him? Well, that depends. If he demands what I can't carry out, then we're both guilty or not guilty. A master must be wise in his way as a servant is in his.

One can imagine what the rejection of his novels must have meant to Walser. He knew that his success as a writer depended on his publishing novels and he had not published one in over a decade.

In Bern he changed residences from one furnished room to another with a frequency mirrored in the rapidity and play of his thought, as seen in the experiments he was undertaking at the time in stories like "Mutterseelenallein," "Book Review," and "Fragment," the latter one of several works by Walser published by Max Brod in the *Prager Presse*, Kafka having enthusiastically recommended Walser's work to his friend over two decades before. Here we see Walser's prose at its most radical, as we do in his final novel, *The Robber*, "a self-portrait and self-examination of absolute incorruptibility" (W. G. Sebald) found after his death on twenty-four octavo-sized pages. The novel is part of the so-called *Mikrogramme*, a trove of 526 scraps of paper written in pencil in a minuscule script on, variously, the backs of calendar pages, envelopes, rejection slips, business cards, advertisements, and the covers of dime novels.

In Bern Walser had eight years of astonishing productivity until on January 24, 1929, suffering from severe psychic stress (nightmares, aural hallucinations, depression, "a few bumbling attempts to take my own life"), at the urging of his sister Lisa, a teacher in Bellelay, he committed himself to Waldau, fearing he would never leave the asylum but believing he would have the right to. Before entering, as he later told the Swiss journalist Carl Seelig, Walser asked Lisa, "'Are we doing the right thing?' Her silence said enough. What choice did I have but to enter?" (Seelig, *Walks with Walser*, trans. Anne Posten, New Directions, 2017).

Walser's familiarity with madness and loss had begun at an early age. In 1885 the oldest of his five brothers, Adolf Emil, died at age fifteen, and his father, Adolf Walser, a merchant, experiencing economic difficulties, had to relocate his business and family to less expensive quarters. At this time his mother, Eliza Marti, suffered a depressive breakdown from which she never fully recovered. A blacksmith's daughter from the Emmental, she died when Walser was sixteen; his father twenty years later, in 1914. Another brother, Ernst, entered Waldau as a patient in 1898 and died there while in a vegetative state in 1916. And in 1919, Hermann, the oldest living brother, a geography professor in Bern—he had seen to Ernst's needs in Waldau, and financed their younger sister Fanny's studies—committed suicide.

In Waldau, Walser soon settled into a routine of gardening and writing, until 1933, when the clinic's new director, the psychiatrist Jakob Klaesi, decided to focus on acute cases and release patients like Walser into the care of a farming family. No farm boy, as Bernhard Echte notes in his comprehensive *Robert Walser: Sein Leben in Bildern und Texten* (Robert Walser: His Life in Pictures and Texts, Suhrkamp, 2008), Walser refused this offer, preferring to move in with Lisa. Neither she nor her school desired this and both worked to have Walser transferred to another clinic. On June 19, with Walser physically resisting, he was taken to the cantonal psychiatric clinic of Appenzell Ausserrhoden (his canton of domicile) in eastern Switzerland, overlooking the town of Herisau.

Only here did he effectively shut down what he called his "little prose-piece shop" (*Prosastückligeschäft*), telling his doctor not to bother him about writing and his former literary life, that it was all far behind him. In *Walks with Walser*, Seelig, who visited Walser throughout most of his years in the Herisau clinic and became his legal guardian, reveals a man whose mental vivacity had not waned. On Christmas Day, 1956, twenty-three years after his removal to Herisau, he died of a heart attack while on a solitary walk on the snow-covered mountains adjacent to the clinic.

OTHER NEW YORK REVIEW CLASSICS

For a complete list of titles, visit www.nyrb.com or write to:
Catalog Requests, NYRB, 435 Hudson Street, New York, NY 10014

RICHARD HUGHES A High Wind in Jamaica
INTIZAR HUSAIN Basti
MAUDE HUTCHINS Victorine
YASUSHI INOUE Tun-huang
DARIUS JAMES Negrophobia: An Urban Parable
HENRY JAMES The New York Stories of Henry James
TOVE JANSSON The Summer Book
TOVE JANSSON The Woman Who Borrowed Memories: Selected Stories
RANDALL JARRELL (EDITOR) Randall Jarrell's Book of Stories
DIANE JOHNSON The True History of the First Mrs. Meredith and Other Lesser Lives
UWE JOHNSON Anniversaries
JOSEPH JOUBERT The Notebooks of Joseph Joubert; translated by Paul Auster
ERNST JÜNGER The Glass Bees
FRIGYES KARINTHY A Journey Round My Skull
ERICH KÄSTNER Going to the Dogs: The Story of a Moralist
ANNA KAVAN Machines in the Head: Selected Stories
YASHAR KEMAL Memed, My Hawk
WALTER KEMPOWSKI All for Nothing
RAYMOND KENNEDY Ride a Cockhorse
ROBERT KIRK The Secret Commonwealth of Elves, Fauns, and Fairies
DEZSŐ KOSZTOLÁNYI Skylark
TÉTÉ-MICHEL KPOMASSIE An African in Greenland
TOM KRISTENSEN Havoc
GYULA KRÚDY The Adventures of Sindbad
SIGIZMUND KRZHIZHANOVSKY Autobiography of a Corpse
SIGIZMUND KRZHIZHANOVSKY Unwitting Street
K'UNG SHANG-JEN The Peach Blossom Fan
D.H. LAWRENCE The Bad Side of Books: Selected Essays
PATRICK LEIGH FERMOR Between the Woods and the Water
PATRICK LEIGH FERMOR The Broken Road
PATRICK LEIGH FERMOR A Time of Gifts
PATRICK LEIGH FERMOR The Traveller's Tree
NIKOLAI LESKOV Lady Macbeth of Mtsensk: Selected Stories of Nikolai Leskov
SIMON LEYS The Hall of Uselessness: Collected Essays
MARGARITA LIBERAKI Three Summers
JAKOV LIND Soul of Wood and Other Stories
H.P. LOVECRAFT AND OTHERS Shadows of Carcosa: Tales of Cosmic Horror
CURZIO MALAPARTE Diary of a Foreigner in Paris
JANET MALCOLM In the Freud Archives
JEAN-PATRICK MANCHETTE Nada
JEAN-PATRICK MANCHETTE No Room at the Morgue
OLIVIA MANNING Fortunes of War: The Balkan Trilogy
JAMES VANCE MARSHALL Walkabout
GUY DE MAUPASSANT Like Death
JAMES McCOURT Mawrdew Czgowchwz
WILLIAM McPHERSON Testing the Current
DAVID MENDEL Proper Doctoring: A Book for Patients and their Doctors
W.S. MERWIN (TRANSLATOR) The Life of Lazarillo de Tormes
MEZZ MEZZROW AND BERNARD WOLFE Really the Blues
HENRI MICHAUX Miserable Miracle
JESSICA MITFORD Hons and Rebels
NANCY MITFORD Voltaire in Love